SYDNEY J. BOUNDS

MURDER IN SPACE

*Complete and Unabridged*

LINFORD
*Leicester*

First published in Great Britain

First Linford Edition
published 2007

British Library CIP Data

Bounds, Sydney J.
    Murder in space.—Large print ed.—
Linford mystery library
    1. Murder—Investigation—Fiction
    2. Astronauts—Fiction
    3. Detective and mystery stories
    4. Large type books
    I. Title
    823.9'14 [F]

    ISBN 978–1–84617–910–5

Published by
F. A. Thorpe (Publishing)
Anstey, Leicestershire

Set by Words & Graphics Ltd.
Anstey, Leicestershire
Printed and bound in Great Britain by
T. J. International Ltd., Padstow, Cornwall

This book is printed on acid-free paper

# MURDER IN SPACE

British Security is alerted when astronaut Peter Bourne suffers two assassination attempts, intended to look like accidents. After Bourne is blasted into space to place a top-secret device in orbit, detective Simon Brand is summoned to investigate, and to protect the device from being stolen. But then Bourne's spacecraft loses radio contact . . . When it returns, the pilot is dead — murdered whilst alone in space, in a sealed ship! So begins one of Brand's most baffling and dangerous cases . . .

# 1

## Fatal flight

He looked like a creature from another world.

He was zipped into a silver-coloured pressure suit of rubber and nylon; an armour against the cold and airless void of space. The visor of his helmet lay open to reveal blunt features permeated with a calculating calmness; hard experience overlying youth.

He was Wing-Commander Peter Bourne, and he was going out into deep space. And he was going into space on a very special mission.

He stood for a long moment in the doorway of the blockhouse, eyes searching the empty concrete landscape ahead. On the horizon towered a three-stage rocket, sheathed in its protective steel gantry. Below, the squat shape of a Landrover moved rapidly towards him.

He checked the faces of the sparse sprinkling of people waiting in the thin, pallid sunshine on the edge of the concrete plain in front of the blockhouse. Mostly, they were minor technicians. Then he saw Bob Frost, the Chief Security Officer and, standing next to Frost, he saw Melanie . . .

A smile warmed Peter Bourne's face at the sight of her and, for a moment, he seemed to shed his load of years, the burden of hours to come. Five-feet-two with short blonde hair, Melanie had an hour-glass figure shoe-horned into an intoxicatingly flimsy dress. Three years married to her, he thought wryly, and still she made his mouth dry and his blood pump faster.

He walked forward, looking straight ahead.

'All right, Peter?' she asked lightly.

'Fine.'

His eyes raked over the Landrover coming towards him and fixed on the man sitting beside the driver. It was Chief Technician Ben Weller. The Land rover stopped in front of them, the engine

2

ticking over. Ben Weller, tall and lanky, angled awkwardly out of the vehicle hefting his tool kit.

Peter Bourne spoke. 'O.K., Ben?'

'Sure,' Weller drawled, eyeing the distant rocket. 'She'll bring you back.'

'Alive, I hope!'

There was no answering smile on Weller's weathered face. Bourne said abruptly: 'Well, time to be going.'

Melanie kissed him. Reaching his lips beyond the projecting visor proved to be difficult, but she managed it. He felt the animal warmth of her body as she strained against him. For a brief moment he knew sadness, and fought it.

He broke away. He looked steadily at Weller. 'Take good care of her, Ben.'

Fractionally, Weller's lips thinned. Then he forced a smile. 'Of course. I'll do that small thing.'

Peter Bourne stepped into the waiting Landrover and the driver swung the vehicle round. Bourne brooded on the run out to the rocket. A near-elusive breath of Melanie's perfume lingered around him, conjuring up all kinds of longings. It had been a mistake to have her see him off . . .

A lift carried him up to the entry port of the rocket, and he wriggled inside. Leg straps. Chest strap. He was thinking mechanically, obeying practised routine. Visor closed. Oxygen on. He lifted a gloved hand to wave to the mechanic poised outside. The entry port slowly closed and the catches latched, locking him away from Earth, from Melanie, from everything.

He was truly alone. And only then did he allow his breath to sigh out in relief. He was safe.

The foam-rubber couch gave under his weight. It would give a lot more when acceleration built up. He had no room for movement. He was buried beneath a maze of cables and instruments attached to a panel of lights and switches. He was a robot.

A disembodied voice came over the radio. 'Countdown starting — now!'

It droned on, even as he made his final test of the control panel.

'Fifty seconds . . . forty . . . thirty . . . twenty . . . '

Pumps thudded rhythmically. Lights flashed. The vibration set his teeth on edge.

'Four ... three ... two ... one ... zero ...

'Fire rockets!' The terrible roar died away behind him. An invisible giant was sitting on his chest, forcing him down into the rubber couch. His face was distorted with multiplying gravity. Vision blurred. Sweat beaded under the visor.

Then there was startling, bottomless silence.

It was silence that deafened him. Pressure eased, and the couch expanded. His gaze flickered over the instruments, and he spoke the readings aloud into a chest microphone.

The second-stage rockets fired, but it was not so bad this time. He reported back to the monitor, far below.

The third stage fired, and he waited breathlessly for the moment of ejection. When it came, he would be a man in space, totally enclosed in the metal nosecone of the rocket.

If anything went wrong with ejection

. . . He tried not to think about it.

If anything went wrong, the cone would be his coffin and more than his coffin. It would be a blazing funeral pyre.

★ ★ ★

She said: 'Please come in, Mr. Brand. He is expecting you.'

Simon Brand smiled pleasantly. Perhaps the brunette thought it a smile of appreciation. She was tall and willowy, with a short black skirt, dark nylons, and a white shirt, the front slashed down in a vee. But Brand's smile meant merely that Kaner never changed . . .

The inner sanctum smelled faintly of aromatic Eastern tobacco. Kaner, head of one of Britain's more important intelligence agencies, waved Brand to a chair. He did not speak at once.

Brand sat down, crossed his legs, and prepared to wait patiently. Kaner had sent for him. It was enough.

The amber eyes stared down at wrinkled parchment hands. The familiar dry voice rustled slowly to life. 'A strange story, Brand. Perhaps important . . . we are putting a man into space on our own account. A British astronaut to follow the Russians and the Americans — we hope.'

Simon Brand looked mildly surprised. 'I thought the government had turned down sending men in space, on account of the cost. Instruments, yes — even crewmen — but as part of foreign missions.'

Kaner nodded. 'They did. And changed their minds — in secret session. Half the money is coming from private industrial sources, both here and in Europe, to pioneer some communication gadget the boffins have dreamed up. The rocket employed has been provided by the United States. So we have a British astronaut, by courtesy of the Americans and European Union big business — a bitter pill for some Little Englanders to swallow. That has made security even more difficult than usual. And now this . . . '

And now this . . . Brand leaned forward, intent on the seamed and wrinkled face.

Kaner coughed. 'He's up there now.' His amber eyes had a far-away look in them. It was as if he spoke his thoughts aloud, as if Brand were not there. 'He's fit; must be. He passed all the medical and psychiatric tests, and God knows there are enough of them. So why would he dream up a story like this . . . ?'

For the first time, Kaner looked squarely at Brand, and raised his voice to a normal level for conversation.

'Wing-Commander Peter Bourne, British astronaut, believes that someone is trying to kill him. He has no evidence to support this belief. No real, concrete evidence; that is. All the same, he says that two attempts have recently been made on his life. Both attempts — he says — have been made to look like accidents.'

Kaner fitted a fat cigarette into a long holder. He pressed a desk lighter, and thoughtfully regarded the flame.

'Something personal?' Brand hazarded. 'Or involving security?'

Kaner smiled bleakly. 'Wing-Commander Bourne doesn't seem to think highly of security. He doesn't know — our

8

connection. I suggested a private investigator. When he lands, I want you to handle it.'

'Any special orders?' Brand asked gently.

'Only one. You've got to move quickly. I must know . . . either he's cracking, or telling a fantastic story for some reason of his own, or it's true. If it's true, we're going to have to move fast.'

Kaner jabbed the air with his long cigarette holder.

'Wing-Commander Bourne represents an important investment in time and money. Also, his space mission is significant in a national sense. I think that — '

But there Kaner stopped, for a buzzer had rasped. Kaner's thin hands moved over the mass of papers on his desk and disinterred a telephone. As he listened, a shadow passed across his face. He replaced the instrument, amber eyes narrowed on the detective.

'Ground monitor reports that Bourne stopped speaking to them in midsentence. I think you'd better get down there right away, Brand!'

The recovery truck swung ponderously along a dried-up water-course, jolting over stones and roots. A wild, desolate landscape stretched to every horizon. This was Dartmoor, bleak with stunted trees and jagged outcrops of rock, sparsely covered with heather and bracken.

The driver muttered under his breath as he tried to keep the drifting silver nosecone in view. It came swinging down from the sky beneath a huge, pale blue canopy.

Then the truck bogged down in marshy ground, the engine revved shrilly and the heavy-duty tyres spun uselessly. Men climbed down and fed planks under the wheels.

Not for the first time, they cursed authority for siting the station in the middle of such difficult terrain.

Somewhere ahead, a Landrover rattled its way over rough ground.

Apart from the driver, three men clung tight-lipped to their seats.

In front, Chief Technician Ben Weller

felt happy. The retro-rockets had worked perfectly, and the nosecone was dropping precisely into the reception area pin-pointed for it.

In the back seat of the Landrover, Bob Frost, the Chief Security Officer, grumbled with each bone-shaking lurch of the vehicle. He was not happy. But his orders were to be present when the nosecone was recovered.

Beside him, Doctor Fenwick thought only of the man inside the nosecone. He had stopped recording. That might mean only a radio fault . . . or it might mean something much worse.

'It's down,' Weller said, the barest trace of excitement in his voice.

No one else spoke. The driver slewed the Landrover through a skidding arc and crammed on speed.

He had his target now. Despite the rough ride, he made fast time.

The spacecraft lay on its side, parachute dragging. Ben Weller was out of the Landrover, carrying his toolkit, almost before the vehicle jolted to a shuddering halt.

He sweated as he unscrewed the catches securing the escape hatch.

The doctor waited patiently to help the man imprisoned inside.

The driver lit a cigarette and stretched his aching muscles. Bob Frost, of Security, scanned the surrounding countryside with high-magnification binoculars. It was the job of his department to keep unauthorised people out of the area, but this was difficult terrain to police satisfactorily. There was always the chance that some undesirable character might have slipped through the cordon. He studied every rock and clump of vegetation very minutely.

'Recovery truck's stuck,' he said absently. 'Won't be here for quite a while.'

He continued his study of the landscape, pausing as the wind stirred the leaves on a distant bush.

Doctor Fenwick watched Ben Weller at work on the catches securing the hatch. The technician was moving fast, conscious that a life may depend on an extra second.

The doctor wet his lips nervously.

What were they going to find inside?

Weller finished, and slid the hatch clear. 'Your meat, doc,' he said cheerfully.

Fenwick craned his head into the confined space; grunted. It was instantly obvious to him that the man inside the nosecone was unconscious. Fenwick tried to reach him, and grunted again. It was worse than trying to get at a trapped man in a rail smash. He drew back, red-faced and gasping.

'He's out for the count. Have to get him clear of that thing to do any good.'

Weller reached through and uncoupled belt fastenings. He got his hands under Bourne's armpits and heaved. He braced himself. They hadn't designed the cone for extracting a helpless man. There was no room to work in.

He lugged Bourne's head and shoulders clear, and struggled to extricate the space pilot's limp arms.

Fenwick got a purchase and, between them, they dragged Peter Bourne out of the nosecone like a cork from a bottle.

Ben Weller squeezed inside the cone. There was one job he had still to do . . .

Doctor Fenwick dropped on one knee at Peter Bourne's side. The pilot was sprawled face down on the moor. His body was limply inert.

The doctor grunted as he rolled him over — then sucked in a sudden sharp breath.

There was a jagged rent in Bourne's spacesuit, at the throat, where some missile had torn a way through. The opening was greasy with black, jellied blood.

Peter Bourne wasn't unconscious.

Peter Bourne, British astronaut, had returned from space . . . dead.

# 2

## Melanie

Simon Brand maintained a high speed along the A-30, driving his MG sports car flat out to reach Devon quickly.

He wasn't alone in his car.

His secretary, the tall, honey-blonde Marla Dean, and his young partner, Nick Chandler, were with him as far as Oakhampton, twenty-six miles north-west of Exeter. There, he stopped in front of the *Wheat Sheaf*, in the High Street, and set them down.

A bare minute later, waving a hasty farewell, Brand was going on; swinging his sports car south on to a new concrete road which plunged straight into the heart of the wild and rugged fastness of Dartmoor.

The detective was only subconsciously aware of the bleak and grimly forbidding country that he passed. His brows were knitted in concentration.

On his left, Yes Tor rose starkly against the skyline, a ragged, jagged towering peak of volcanic rock a hundred million years old. Closer at hand, a landmark of more recent origin was a boldly-lettered sign-board facing the road: *BEWARE — DANGER ZONE — ARTILLERY PRACTICE.*

But Brand did not slacken his speed.

He didn't stop until, a few miles farther on, the concrete road ended abruptly before a high fence and a checkpoint under another sign that read: *INTERCONTINENTAL COMMUNICATIONS.* And here a uniformed security guard examined the pass that Kaner had supplied, before saluting and directing the detective onward.

'The first building on your left, sir. Mr. Frost, the Chief Security Officer, is expecting you.'

Brand pulled up outside a low, prefabricated hut. Neatly lettered on the door was the single word: *SECURITY.* He swung himself out of his car and pushed open the door of the hut to hear angry voices.

'What you're saying, doctor, is just too fantastic for words! Bourne was up there alone. It just can't be murder!'

Brand took a swift, but silent, pace forward. Now he could see the hut's occupants. And his eyes focused sharply on the portly, ruddy-faced man who, in reply, was thrusting something forward in a fat, podgy hand.

'Frost, this says it was murder! I'm willing to stake my reputation on the fact that it was this that killed him. And just look at it! It's a flattened bullet if ever I saw one. I — '

But there the portly man stopped. He had just become aware of Brand's presence. Simultaneously, the other two men in the room wheeled around.

One of them, angry-eyed, snapped at Brand: 'Who the hell are you?'

Brand offered the pass Kaner had given him.

'Oh, I see . . . well, I'm Bob Frost. This is one hell of a mess . . . '

Brand's gaze rested briefly on the Chief Security Officer. Frost didn't look happy. His pale brown eyes were very worried indeed. He tugged nervously at his ragged moustache.

'Doctor Fenwick,' he said, gesturing in the direction of the other men in the hut. He indicated the portly man first. 'Doctor Fenwick. And Ben Weller, our number one technician.'

Brand nodded, looking thoughtfully at the doctor's closed hand. 'Mind if I see your evidence, doctor?' he asked mildly.

Doctor Fenwick glanced at Frost, who growled: 'It's all right. More security.' Bitterness entered his voice. 'Apparently I'm no longer trusted. Those desk boys in London don't realise just how tough a job this is.'

Fenwick opened his hand, and Brand cautiously picked up a flattened lump of lead.

'That's what killed Peter Bourne,' the doctor stated. 'It was fired into his neck at close range. It was bullet-shaped when it was fired. It flattened on impact. I'm almost willing to bet it was a bullet.'

Brand weighed the lump of lead thoughtfully.

'It punched clean through Bourne's

throat,' the doctor went on, 'tearing it open and slicing the carotid artery. Death resulted almost immediately from severe loss of blood.'

Bob Frost edged a finger under his collar; loosened it. 'I don't see how you can be so sure he was killed by that thing,' he complained. 'I just don't see it. You didn't find it anywhere near Peter Bourne's body.'

'Maybe not. But I still say it killed him.' Fenwick was obstinate. 'It was covered with blood when I found it.'

'So were a lot of other things in the nosecone.'

'Surprisingly few,' Fenwick said stubbornly. 'Bourne bled into his spacesuit. In any case, none of the other things was of this size and weight. And it must have been something of this size and weight that killed Bourne. You can't get away from it.'

'But — but couldn't he have been killed by — well — well by a meteorite, say?'

Frost was beginning to sound desperate.

19

Simon Brand returned the flattened lead slug to the doctor. The lanky technician, Weller, had not spoken yet — but his gaze was fixed, almost hypnotically, on the detective.

Brand said slowly: 'I suppose the Security Officer has a point. Shall we inspect the spacecraft for signs of penetration?'

Then Weller spoke. 'You won't find any.' He sounded quite certain.

Frost glared at him. 'We'll take a look, anyway.'

He led the way across bare concrete to a steel shed. Inside, under fluorescent lights, Brand saw the spacecraft that had taken Peter Bourne in an orbit of Earth. It looked puny; almost insignificant.

It was barely twice the height of a man. Halfway down its brief length, a circular port lay open.

On a workbench, Bourne's spacesuit had been laid out, like some obscene, deflated corpse. Brand studied the gashed neck of the suit. Whatever missile had killed Bourne had struck from the left side.

He stepped over to the nosecone and craned his head inside, studying the pilot's position. Then his eyes scanned the interior of the cone. He went over it carefully. There was no hole in the spacecraft.

But there was a small cylinder fixed to the interior of the cone. It was a cylinder about six inches in length and of about one and a half inches diameter. And one end of it pointed ominously . . .

Brand withdrew his head and called Weller. He pointed. 'What's that?'

'Compressed air. For operating one of the instruments.'

Compressed air . . . Brand exchanged a glance with Doctor Fenwick. The same thought had occurred to both men. Compressed air could be used to fire a lead slug.

'Has anyone been inside the cone since it landed?' he asked, turning to Frost.

'Only Ben Weller. He was the last man in before Bourne went up. He's the only one of us who's been inside it since it landed.'

'My job,' Weller drawled. 'I fitted

Professor Colman's communicator before launching. I removed it as soon as the cone returned from orbit. You may or may not know it, but the professor's little gadget is the reason for the existence of this entire enterprise. And I look after it. That little gadget is extremely important. Normally it's kept under lock and key.'

Brand climbed into the cone and seated himself where Bourne had been a few hours previously. He tried to imagine what it had been like — locked in, alone out there in space. And death had struck suddenly, unexpectedly. Abruptly, he remembered that Bourne had claimed someone was trying to kill him.

'Pass me a spanner, Weller,' he said.

The technician grinned broadly. He pulled a spanner from his pocket and handed it through the open hatch. It exactly fitted the nuts holding the miniscule air cylinder to its bracket.

Ben Weller appeared to be enjoying some joke of his own as, with a few deft turns, Brand loosened the nuts and removed the cylinder and passed it out to Frost. Brand didn't quite know what to make of Weller. The man must realise he was suspect . . .

Brand wriggled clear of the cone, and stripped down the cylinder on the workbench. It was a perfectly ordinary compressed air container. There was nothing remarkable about it, except its small size. And Brand knew it could never have been used as a murder weapon.

Behind him, Weller began to laugh.

Frost exploded: 'You've nothing to laugh about, Weller. I think I understand you now . . . it's no secret you were making a play for Bourne's wife.'

For the first time, Brand saw Weller roused. A nerve pulsed in his throat, and his fingers curled. His voice jerked out thickly.

'Damn you, leave Melanie out of it!'

He wheeled on Brand, then checked himself. His anger died. He studied the tall, lean figure of the detective and found something in Brand's blue-grey eyes that calmed him and lent him confidence.

'Now it's my turn to tell some home truths,' he said. 'Security here is a laugh. A blind man could see anything he wanted! And the stuff we're working on is vitally important. It's Britain's — and Europe's — biggest asset.

'If you want to know what I think — it's about time somebody checked up on this character here, our Chief Security Officer, Mister Frost. There's a certain redhead called Marilyn Martin who twists him round her little finger! You should ask her a few questions. And, while you're about it, check on Bourne's associates. Maybe you'll get a few surprises!'

Weller's voice was harsh, accusing.

'You follow me, Brand? Professor Colman's invention has immense commercial value, and we can't afford to let it fall into the wrong hands! This country certainly needs a boost, and Colman's little gadget could help put us on our feet. But — believe me! — it's certainly time we had some real security here! Or are you someone else who thinks it's out of date to be patriotic?'

Brand was stunned by the vehemence of the man. Weller's teeth showed and his hands were knotted, and his voice had almost risen to shouting pitch.

This was not the speech of a murderer trying to clear himself.

Bob Frost, a shade paler, spoke quickly.

'You understand, Mr. Brand, that with a set-up like this — only partially government-controlled — security could never be all we would like.'

Weller's lips curled.

Brand's own mouth tightened a fraction.

Then he said: 'I think I'd like to meet Peter Bourne's widow now.'

★　★　★

The colour had drained from Melanie's face. And the black, tailored two-piece suit that she wore emphasised her unnatural pallor.

The suit moulded itself to her excellent figure, and Brand did not have to use any imagination to appreciate that Melanie Bourne would be a target for every hot-blooded male within striking distance.

He sat at ease in the lounge of a station prefab. It was comfortably, not luxuriously, furnished; yet he detected certain anomalies.

For one thing, he could see a beautiful reliquary cross of cloisonnee enamel. Nearby was an exquisitely carved ivory plaque. Elsewhere in the room there was a faded silk hanging bearing a magnificent eagle. And all of these things were undoubtedly very old, and very valuable. Could they be family heirlooms?

Every piece was Byzantine in origin.

'I must apologise for intruding at this time,' he said quietly.

Melanie Bourne stood with flowers behind her, one hand braced on a polished table. Only a certain rigidity in the way that she stood betrayed emotion. She kept herself under control, for which Brand was grateful. A hysterical woman would be an embarrassment now.

'Of course, I understand,' she said. 'There must be questions.' Melanie Bourne's voice held a desperate plea. 'Tell me what happened. I know that he's dead; nothing else. They would not even let me see him.'

Brand watched her eyes as he spoke. 'Your husband was murdered, Mrs. Bourne.'

The azure-blue eyes opened wide. He read only stupefied astonishment in them.

'Murdered . . . ? But . . . but I don't understand. He was alone . . . wasn't he?'

Brand nodded. 'Technically, it was a very clever murder.'

She struggled with the idea. 'But who . . . ?'

'Exactly! And to help me answer that question I was hoping that you might suggest a motive.'

She did not reply. Her surprise was genuine, Brand thought. She hadn't taken it in yet.

He said, 'Ben Weller has been mentioned. Apparently, he is infatuated with you.'

'Ben Weller — ?' She appeared startled. 'That's ridiculous! Oh, yes, he's in love with me, but . . . you see, Mr. Brand, I happened to love my husband.'

He allowed a thin silence to settle between them before he inquired delicately 'You've been married three years. You have no children?'

She remained calm, but a shadow of pain showed in her eyes. 'No. It was

27

impossible. Peter . . . my husband . . . not me.'

A motive for murder, Brand wondered. Melanie Bourne looked the maternal type. Just how badly did she want a child? Desperately enough to seek out a father? Weller for instance?

'Tell me about your husband's friends,' he prompted. 'I don't mean his colleagues on this station. You must have had other friends . . . gone out to parties. In Oakhampton, possibly?'

'No parties. Not lately. Peter sometimes went out alone. We . . . that is, Peter, seemed to have changed. Only in the past few months. I don't know what went wrong.'

'Weller — ?'

'Oh, no!' And, briefly, her voice was hard; it was brittle. The repeated suggestion was angering her. 'I told you, Mr. Brand. I never played around.' She repeated it. 'I loved my husband.'

Simon Brand rose to his feet. He paced the carpet; allowed his gaze to rest momentarily on the Byzantine plaque. He deliberately infused a note of grimness

28

into his voice. 'So we're back to the question of security . . .'

Mrs. Bourne lifted her head. 'I have Russian blood. Surely they told you that?'

'Technically, you're a British national. Security checks things like that pretty thoroughly. Your great grandparents fled Russia at the time of the Bolshevik revolution.'

Her eyes flashed. 'But you still can't be sure, can you?'

Brand extracted a cigarette from his case; lit it. Deliberately, he didn't answer her. Instead, he asked another question. 'Did your husband mention earlier attempts on his life?'

Again her eyes widened. And again Brand was sure that she wasn't acting. So Peter Bourne hadn't confided in her . . .

Abruptly, he said, 'What do you know about the work going on here?'

'Nothing.' Her voice was positive. 'We learn not to ask questions. Always, it is security. Peter was a rocket pilot. Beyond that, I knew nothing and wanted to know nothing.'

Brand drew on his cigarette and

watched the smoke curl lazily in a sunbeam slanting through the window.

'Was he happy about his job?'

'No.' Again she was positive. 'He got the job by accident. He was commissioned in the Royal Air Force, and seconded for special duties. This he accepted. But what he really wanted to do was to leave the Service and enter commerce. Peter always saw himself as a big business tycoon.'

Brand sighed. He ground out his half-smoked cigarette in a glass ashtray. His brain was busy with unspoken questions. He was plagued with questions, when what he really wanted were answers.

He said, 'That'll be all for now, Mrs. Bourne. Thank you.'

As Simon Brand closed the door behind him, he paused. Now that she was alone, Melanie Bourne had relaxed her rigid grip on herself.

All the barriers were down.

Standing there, Brand heard her sobbing broken-heartedly. And he sighed again.

# 3

## Murder on the moor

'I'll leave her to you, Nick,' Marla Dean said.

Nick Chandler smiled wryly. 'Yes, you do that. I work better without a chaperone!'

Simon Brand's two chief operatives were in the lounge of the *Wheat Sheaf* in Oakhampton, with loose instructions to listen to gossip and watch for anyone interested in the research station on the Moor. Sam, the barman, had pointed out the redhead and hinted that she was more than a good friend to one of the top men at Intercontinental Communications, and that she seemed to have more than her share of feminine curiosity.

So Marla slipped quietly out of the lounge and went to her room, leaving a clear field for Nick.

He made no attempt to hurry the

contact. There were few people in the lounge, and he took his time over finishing a half-pint of bitter, studying the redhead in a convenient mirror.

She sat alone on a high, red-topped chromium stool against the bar counter, her legs crossed and her short tan skirt inched up above her knees, showing long shapely legs clad in sheer nylon.

One of her feet tapped absently, rhythmically, drawing attention to stylish shoes with very high heels.

Her short skirt was taut across her hips. Above the skirt she wore a pale green sweater with a severe neckline.

Nick stepped lightly up to the bar and put down his empty glass beside her.

'Same again, Sam,' he murmured to the barman, and then turned to the redhead with a smile. 'Will you join me, Miss Martin?'

She removed a cigarette from her moist red mouth and frowned at him. Nick grinned back cheerfully.

Then: 'I don't think I know you,' the redhead said coldly.

Nick acted the wolf. 'Don't be like that!

We don't have to be introduced. My name's Chandler, and your name I know. How — ? I made it my business to find out. It isn't often a man sees a lovely girl like you on her own. You're a model, of course. With that face and figure, you must be.'

But this line didn't get any reaction.

Nick got the feeling that he wasn't using the right approach. Marilyn Martin's expression was hard and unyielding. Besides, his enthusiasm had begun to waver a little. In close-up, the redhead's glamour had evaporated slightly. She was older than she had looked from a distance, and had an air of having been around quite a bit. She certainly knew all the answers, Nick thought, and probably quite a few questions that hadn't even occurred to him yet. And her perfume was distinctly overpowering.

'Staying in the hotel?' Nick murmured. 'I wouldn't have thought there'd be much scope for your kind of work in Oakhampton.'

She smiled a brittle smile, emptied her glass and pushed it at Sam. The barman refilled it automatically, and Nick paid.

'Well, cheers,' he said.

Her eyes glittered as she stubbed out her cigarette. Her voice was edged with harshness. 'I've retired from the game,' she said. 'I've a friend down here.'

'Lucky man,' Nick drawled. 'Someone from the station?'

'That'd be telling . . .'

The conversation drifted.

* * *

Sometime later, the redhead glanced at a gold wristwatch, drained her glass at a gulp, and slid off her stool, smoothing her skirt down over her hips. It was a highly professional movement . . . if a little unsteady.

She had had quite a few drinks, all paid for by Nick, and now they were beginning to show their effect.

She stood by the bar, swaying slightly, and her speech was slurred. 'Goin' up t'my room,' she announced. 'Goin' t'lie down.'

She didn't look as if she could navigate

her way across the floor of the lounge unaided, let alone reach her room, and Nick put a hand under her arm. 'Like some help?'

She looked at him in tipsy calculation, then suddenly giggled. 'You wan'to help me to lie down? You naughty man!'

'All I want to do is help you up to your room.'

'Tha's what you say now. Tha's what they all say . . . '

But she let Nick pilot her out of the lounge and into the lift. He helped her out on her landing, and opened her door for her with the key that she fumblingly gave him.

She didn't appear to notice that, after opening the door, he dropped the key into his own pocket.

Then he steadied her as, waveringly, she charted an uncertain course over the threshold. The room was dark, and somehow — Nick never quite knew how it happened — the door was knocked shut before he could locate the light switches. He fumbled around in the stygian blackness. And then —

One moment she was there, somewhere beside him, being held up by his arm . . . the next moment, she wasn't. And there was the dullest of thuds. What had happened?

Had she fallen flat on her face? Had she hurt herself?

Nick hoped not.

In a way, he felt more than a little responsible for her well-being. He hadn't done anything to prevent her getting herself into this state.

With the best will in the world he had let her get tight in the hope that she might let slip something of value in an unguarded moment. Something of value to the current investigation and to Simon Brand.

But she hadn't. She'd just got tipsier and tipsier.

Well, Nick thought as he bent down in the dark and started fumbling around, looking for her, at least he'd pocketed the key to her room without her being aware of the fact. He'd take an impression of it before 'finding' it in the corridor and handing it in to reception. He'd have a duplicate made. Then, at some future time if need be, her room could be searched when she wasn't in it.

Fine.

But where was she now?

Then, suddenly, Nick knew where she was — as he pitched forward, off-balance. He had found her. Or she had found him.

In the darkness, he sprawled across an extra-thick, fleecy-piled rug and tasted her soft mouth on his. Her hands cradled his head — until one was gently withdrawn. There was nothing clumsy in the movement at all.

She kissed him again, more urgently now, and he could feel the heat of her body as she pressed herself hard against him.

And time passed.

Later, she spoke lazily out of the darkness. 'You can keep the key,' she said. 'Come again.'

★ ★ ★

Simon Brand sat behind a desk in the Security Office of Intercontinental Communications.

The office was almost bare. There was just the desk behind which Brand sat, a telephone, two chairs, and a green filing cabinet. A pin-up calendar was the only personal thing in view. Bob Frost of Security seemed to have a predilection for voluptuous redheads with scanty covering.

On the opposite side of the desk to Simon Brand, Ben Weller lit a cigarette. The two men were alone, and Brand wasn't hurrying his interrogation of the technician. While he kept Weller occupied, Frost was searching for the murder weapon.

Searching stores, the workshops, Weller's own quarters . . .

Brand said gently, 'How close were you to Peter Bourne? Did he tell you two attempts had been made on his life?'

Weller stirred in his chair, his weathered face showing mild interest. 'No, he didn't say anything about that to me.'

'What kind of man was he?'

Weller shrugged. 'Just a man.'

'Good at his job?'

Weller shrugged again. 'I suppose so. Not that he was much interested in being a rocket pilot.'

'Oh . . . ?' Brand had heard this before — and recently. But he gave no sign of it. 'What was he interested in?'

'Getting out of the Service.' Ben Weller gave a short laugh. 'He had ideas about becoming a big business tycoon.'

Brand considered this reply thoughtfully. Melanie Bourne had said the same thing, in almost the same words; a fact which once again spotlighted interesting lines of conjecture.

Brand looked carefully at the man on the other side of the desk.

Weller was still young to hold the position he did. He had a strong aquiline face with the intense eyes of a fanatic. An unusual face.

And it was unusual for technical men to hold strong views in favour of security, too. More often than not, they resented the restrictions that it imposed.

Brand's voice was reflective. 'You said you were worried about the station's security arrangements . . .'

'I was. But I'm not any more.' Weller forced a grin. 'You have quite a reputation, Mr. Brand! Maybe I've got a thing about security — but I don't like to see this country short-changed. And security has been slack here . . . you'll find that out for yourself.'

'This woman you mentioned . . . Marilyn Martin. Any special reason for having doubts about her? After all, even security officers are human.'

Weller turned in his seat and nodded at the calendar on the wall.

'That's her . . . Marilyn Martin. Pin-up modelling is her speciality. But wait till you see her. She's the kind who always gets what she wants. Looking at that picture you'd just say she was a nice piece of crumpet. But, believe me, underneath she's as hard as nails and twice as dangerous. And Frost's been neglecting his duties because of her. If he's not around to supervise the guards, they'll get slack too. See what I mean?'

Brand gave the redheaded girl on the calendar his attention. The photograph gave a full view of her figure, but left her face in shadow. Anyway, he knew better than to try to read character from a touched-up glamour print.

Investigating the lush Marilyn Martin could be a job for Nick. Brand smiled at the thought.

He said to Weller: 'Bob Frost suggested that you were making a play for Peter Bourne's wife. What have you got to say about that?'

Weller made a wry face. 'You've met her. Who wouldn't be interested? But she doesn't play around.'

Again Brand noticed the almost identical words used by Weller and Melanie Bourne. Had they concocted a story between them?

He leaned back in his chair and asked, 'Can you tell me something about the new communications device that Peter Bourne was testing?'

Weller shook his head vigorously.

'Not me! You'll have to see Professor Colman about that.'

'I shall,' Brand replied calmly, and then he paused briefly before going on: 'Is there anything else you'd like to tell me, Mr. Weller?'

The technician took his time about answering. He seemed to be considering his words very carefully.

'There's just one point that may have got overlooked. The space capsule could be manually controlled — and would have been if Bourne had lived. That was to be part of the test. In the end, of course, with Bourne dead inside it, it landed on automatics.'

'Manually operated . . . ' Brand mused thoughtfully, eyes half-closed. 'So . . . ?'

Ben Weller shrugged again. 'You figure it out!' He moved restlessly. 'If that's all, I've some unfinished business in Oakhampton. Assuming that it's all right for me to leave the station.'

Brand lifted one black eyebrow sardonically. 'Why not?' he parried.

Frost wouldn't like it. But Marla or Nick could keep a watch on Weller.

'Why not?' Brand repeated. 'If you want to run into town, go right ahead.'

Brand left the Security Office behind Weller. They moved in the same direction, across the wide, floodlit concrete plain beyond the hut.

Brand's gaze roved over a brilliantly illuminated steel gantry in the distance, where overalled men were hard at work — and would work through the night — to prepare another rocket for launching. Closer at hand, he saw the neat rows of prefabs: the technicians' homes. This was a tight little community, a small private world existing in isolation. Petty jealousies had a way of building up into feuds in such circumstances . . .

And there was the wire: the high, floodlit fence shutting them off from the rest of the world. A man might well get tensed-up living behind wire. He might go into town and take that extra drink which would loosen his tongue.

Brand was glad he had played his hunch and planted Nick and Marla in the *Wheat Sheaf* at Oakhampton.

Weller was barely ten yards ahead of Brand, moving with easy, long-legged strides, his footsteps echoing emptily off the concrete plain. They were both walking close to the wire; beyond lay the Moor, dark, windswept and desolate, empty of life.

Then suddenly, startlingly, there was a jagged flash of flame out in the darkness beyond the wire. The sound of a shot followed instantly. Ten yards ahead of Brand, Weller was punched sideways. He fell on his face.

For a split second, Brand could only stand, could only stare, frozen into shocked and incredulous immobility. Then he was running.

He sprinted forward. He reached Weller where he sprawled on the concrete.

One look at the man was enough.

A bullet had ploughed into him with incredible force. It had torn a great gaping hole in his back where it had passed through his body.

Brand dropped to one knee and, hoping against hope, felt for a pulse — but in vain.

Whoever had gunned Ben Weller down had been an accurate shot.

Ben Weller was indubitably dead.

# 4

## Enter Vogel

Brand did not waste another moment.

There was nothing that he, or anyone else, could do for Ben Weller — except see him decently buried.

That could be done . . . and one other thing.

As other men came running up, alarmed by the sound of the shot and a long-distance view of what had happened, Brand leapt to scale the tall wire fence.

The hidden marksman who had gunned Weller down could be apprehended and brought to trial for murder — perhaps. Certainly, Brand would do his utmost to bring this about. And at least he had marked down the position of the gun-flash in the darkness.

Now he sprang at the wire fence and hauled himself upward, shouting out to the other men over his shoulder, telling them to get Frost, the Chief Security Officer, and turn out the guard. The unknown gunman was somewhere out there in the dark night shrouding the Moor, and Frost might be able to throw a quick cordon round the whole area.

Just the same, Brand wasn't inclined to waste time waiting for Frost to act, nor was he going to squander it reaching the Moor the circuitous way, through the main gate of the station.

The close mesh of the fence provided few footholds, and the mass of barbed strands running along the top had been designed to discourage people from climbing over. But Brand managed it in record time.

He dropped down on the other side, pointed himself in the direction from which the gun-flash had come, and he ran.

The ground was hard and uneven.

The killer could still be under cover, waiting for him. Brand felt sorry that he was not carrying his Luger.

He felt exposed, a significant target against the glare of the floodlights behind him. He put his faith in speed and swerved from side to side.

The Moor was silent but for the rustle of withered grass stirred by the wind. He reached a clump of bushes he had earmarked for investigation, and circled warily. Then, at his feet, there was a tiny tinkle of metal. He reached down and picked up an empty cartridge case.

It was still warm.

★ ★ ★

A chill ran along Simon Brand's spine. He was more conscious of his exposed position than ever. The killer could be lurking within feet of him, watching him, waiting for him, playing with him.

But Brand didn't falter.

Carefully, very carefully now, he went over every inch of the ground in the immediate vicinity. He investigated every bush, every fold in the earth, every serap of possible cover.

There was no one there.

He didn't find the killer . . . but he did find something else close to where he had come upon the empty cartridge case.

And as men fanned out from the station and started coming towards him, spread out like beaters scouring the ground, Brand tried to evaluate just what it was that he had discovered.

In one or two places, the long coarse grass had been disturbed. Just barely, faintly disturbed. It was as if it had been laid briefly back and then allowed to spring up again. The casual eye would have seen nothing. But Brand's eye was never casual, and at this moment he was looking hard for the slightest clue.

No man could have laid back the grass so lightly in passing. Brand noted his own progress. It was immediately obvious. Where he had been, the grass had been crushed under his weight.

He deliberately set out to imitate the strange marks, and he failed completely.

He was baffled.

Who — or what — had made these marks? They meant something. They had to. The killer had left them ... and vanished into the darkness.

Brand was still thinking hard when Bob

Frost, the Chief Security Officer, came stumbling over the Moor. And Frost was a very worried, and frightened, man.

'Did you see him, Brand? Which way did he go?'

The security chief panted up looking like a harassed, middle-aged civil servant.

'A damnable thing! Poor Ben! I — I just can't understand it.' A querulous note had entered his voice. 'First the business about Peter Bourne and — and now this — '

Brand interrupted. 'You've put out a general alarm?'

'Of course. Did you see him?'

Brand shook his head. 'No.'

Frost worried his straggling moustache. 'And the Moor's a big place with plenty of cover. There's not really much hope.'

He shouted to his men, telling them to spread out, and then turned back to Brand.

'The police are on their way. It's a terrible business. Terrible!' For a moment, Frost's pale brown eyes regarded Brand accusingly. 'Pity you didn't see him or catch up with him.'

Brand said quietly, but very distinctly, 'I think so, too. But maybe I will.'

He nodded to Frost, and left the security chief and his men to their thankless task.

He was looking thoughtful as he returned to the research station. Very thoughtful indeed.

★  ★  ★

Although she had nominally gone to her room in the *What Sheaf*, Marla Dean had still managed to keep some sort of an eye on Nick, and she had seen him go upstairs with the redhead.

Marla Dean frowned.

Marilyn Martin had impressed her as being a dangerous type. She wondered: what was Nick up to?

She took a shower and changed into a cool, lime-green cocktail dress. And then she heard the car arrive. The driver swung hard into the kerb outside the hotel to avoid a local lunatic on a motorcycle. Tyres shrilled in protest. Marla crossed to the window and glanced out and down.

Then she stared.

The car was a huge black limousine. It was unmistakably a Daimler. But Marla had never, ever, seen its equal before. It was absolutely enormous: long, low, and wide.

It was a custom-built model, obviously, and a car for a man much less concerned with performance charted as so many miles to the gallon than with it expressed as so many gallons per super-luxurious mile.

Marla swallowed hastily. She had caught herself gaping as she watched the vast car disgorge an oddly assorted group of six people, all of whom entered the hotel.

Marla's professional curiosity prompted her to investigate, and she descended in the lift. A guttural voice growled echoingly through the reception hall. Marla spoke briefly to the duty porter.

'Did Mr. Chandler leave any message for me?'

The porter stared at her, distracted. 'No, miss. No message.'

Marla had a back view of the owner of

the guttural growl and the gargantuan car as he waddled into the lounge bar followed by his entourage. Marla was fascinated. Working as Simon Brand's private secretary, she met all kinds of people. But she had never seen anything like this — except on a film set.

The leader of the party was a good yard in front of the others. He was an immense man-mountain of Savile Row-tailored, bald, quivering flesh. And, as he went, his harsh guttural growl was flung back over his shoulder. 'Can't waste time . . . time's money . . .'

His greedy, grossly fat fingers, like two pounds of pink, over-plump pork sausages on the end of each arm, clenched and unclenched with every growled word.

Behind him paced three slim-shouldered, narrow-hipped men in City-type charcoal grey suits and bowlers. They were alike in almost every particular. All three were tall, all three were young, and all three had hard, unsmiling faces. Their pale eyes raked the hotel scene.

And behind them wiggled two young and physically-ripe girls, one blonde, one brunette, gracing Park Lane dresses and exuding perfume created by the House of Chanel. They were the starlet type, Marla thought. They were that type of contract artiste who could be relied on to brighten any producer's lonely, dull evening.

Their lord and master had reached the bar, and there he paused to stare bleakly around him. The barman caught the full blast of the grossly fat man's cold, basilisk gaze, and swallowed numbly. 'Yes, sir . . . ?' he got out.

But the grossly fat man did not deign to answer.

Instead, he gestured curtly and turned away, and one of his three, slim, City-suited henchmen slid swiftly forward. 'Mr. Vogel is looking for a Mister Len Rushton. Is he here?'

The barman's gaze jumped nervously from one man to the other: from the dangerously slim to the cruelly fat. Then he swallowed again. 'Sorry, sir. Mr. Rushton's not in the hotel at the moment.'

'Get the manager,' the immensely obese man growled in the background.

'We'll need four suites of rooms.'

'Mr. Vogel wants the manager,' the man in the charcoal-grey suit told the barman shortly. 'Where is he?'

The manager arrived with a professional dry-wash of hands and an expression of deepest regret. 'I'm sorry, sir. We're fully booked.'

The grossly fat man called Vogel regarded him bleakly but didn't speak. At his elbow Vogel's henchman said coldly, '*You're* sorry . . . Mr. Vogel's sorry too. He's come all the way from London. That's quite a way for Mr. Vogel to come to find a hotel with no rooms free. Mr. Vogel's not very pleased. Who owns this hotel? Maybe he'll buy it.'

The manager gulped.

'I — I don't think that would be possible, sir. May I suggest . . . '

But, at a curt nod from his obese overlord, Vogel's henchman turned his back on the manager; turned back to the bar.

'A large brandy for Mr. Vogel. And two gin-slings.' He extracted a banknote from a bulging wallet and tossed the note on to the counter. 'And Mr. Vogel says have something yourself. Keep the change.'

The order was speedily filled.

Marla noted that none of the three City-suited hatchet men in bowler hats had a drink. And now they faded discreetly into the background.

On the other hand, the two starlets lapped up their gin-slings like kittens at a milk bowl. And Vogel downed his brandy at a gulp and then turned and Marla got her first view of the man's face in close-up.

It was a thick-lipped, cruel face and the heavily pouched eyes were icy-blue gimlets that bored into her without friendliness even as the mouth smiled.

Vogel's voice was a purr now. 'Forgive me, my dear. But perhaps you can help me. You heard . . . ? I'm looking for a man called Rushton. Len Rushton. You'll know him if you are connected with the space project which is taking shape around here.'

'I've not had the pleasure of meeting your friend,' Marla said. And Vogel's mouth lost its smile.

'He's no friend of mine! He's pig-headed and obstinate. He could change things. It's in his power. But he won't.' Vogel's voice had risen, and now it shook angrily.

'Always his answer is no. He says no to me!'

Plainly, Vogel found this almost beyond belief.

Then, suddenly, his mouth smiled again, but grimly this time: a cruel, shark's smile, He said softly, 'But he'll learn. Oh, yes, never fear, he'll certainly learn. I can be very obstinate myself. If I make up my mind I want a thing, nothing stops me. I get it . . . '

And now his eyes were wandering over Marla.

In a thick, honied purr, he said, 'But that's enough about me. And enough about Rushton, too. Quite enough. Let's talk about you, my dear, for a moment. You're not connected with the space project? No . . . ? Then — forgive me asking, my dear — what do you do?'

'I'm a secretary,' Marla said.

Vogel's greedy eyes continued to linger

over her excellent figure. She felt as if she was being leisurely undressed, garment by garment, Vogel said, 'A secretary, eh? But not here. Not in this remote district.'

'No,' Marla agreed. 'I just happen to be here on business.'

'With your employer ... of course,' Vogel said, and chuckled suggestively.

Marla could have hit him.

Then, abruptly, his gaze snapped up to meet hers.

'Well, my dear,' he purred, 'I might have a job for you in my organisation, should you ever want one. A good job. Very well paid. You'd like it.'

He chuckled again, a horrible sound.

Then: 'My card,' he said, and without taking his eyes off her face he extended a hand sideways and snapped obscenely fat fingers. Instantly, one of his bowler-hatted City-suited retainers appeared out of nowhere to slip an expensively engraved rectangle of pasteboard between them.

Without change of expression, Vogel held the card out to Marla Dean. 'Here you are, my dear. Look me up.'

Then, suddenly, he was glancing at a

solid gold wristwatch and grunting. 'Excuse me. I've got to chase this Rushton man now.'

He waddled away, an obese Napoleon of very big business. His entourage took station behind him, the three hard-eyed hatchet men in City suits, the two sprightly starlets.

Marla followed them out into the hall. She let her breath slowly.

'Well . . . '

She stared at the rectangle of pasteboard she still held in her hand. Brand would want to know about Mr. Vogel.

The immensely fat man had impressed her as one who usually got what he wanted. He would be a man not easily deterred or distracted; a man not easily stopped.

# 5

## Ramifications

'Security . . . ? You're concerned with Security . . . ? Then why don't you take yourself off and concern yourself with it? Why come badgering me?'

There was a growl of impatience in the voice of the man who now faced Simon Brand.

The detective had urgently sought, and finally obtained, an interview with the principal scientist at the research station: Professor Julian Colman.

Brand perched on a wooden stool in a long, low laboratory. Fluorescent lighting blazed down on spotless benches; air extractors hummed quietly in the background. Despite a prominently-displayed 'No Smoking' notice, the professor puffed at a thin, black cheroot. He was the key man on the station, and a law unto himself.

A slight, dapper figure with a wisp of beard straggling from a long jaw, Colman strode briskly up and down, gesticulating with stubby fingers. 'I have better things to do than waste time answering a string of damn-fool questions!'

Following the professor's progress, Brand was in danger of getting Wimbledon neck.

'Nevertheless,' he put in then, quietly but firmly, 'two men on the strength of this station have died violently within the last twenty-four hours. First Bourne, and now Weller. You must appreciate my position, professor. I need to know what's going on here to determine whether or not the two murders share a common motive. I'm not asking for classified information, merely to be put in the picture generally.'

And Colman snorted.

'Classified poppycock! If I told you — in exact mathematical terms — what you're asking me to tell you, you'd be no wiser. In general terms, you've read it all in the papers, or should have. It's no secret — in general terms.'

'I'd still like to hear your version,' Brand said quietly. 'Newspapers sometimes garble scientific reports.'

Colman snorted again, but then conceded the truth of this grudgingly. 'Very well . . . '

He continued to pace the laboratory, only pausing to light a fresh cheroot. Did he realise, Brand wondered, that he was virtually a prisoner on the research station?

'In general terms, Mr. Brand . . . in association with the European Union countries, we are putting a satellite into space. The satellite will act as a space relay. A relay for a radio-telecommunications system . . . among other things.

'In general terms, again, I need only give you one example of the value of this aspect of the relay's capabilities.

'Way back in nineteen fifty-six, the first transatlantic telephone cable was laid, and it carried thirty-six channels. Previous to that, undersea cables carried telegraph signals only. Long-distance radio depended on our bouncing short waves off the reflective ionosphere layer, and was not exactly reliable.

'These days things have changed. By going into space, we get a broadband transoceanic link — direct and without interference. My relay aboard the satellite will carry several *million* conversations simultaneously. With three such stations, suitably positioned in orbit, we achieve worldwide coverage. The perfect communications system! And this is not all. But . . . ' he paused . . . 'I think I've said enough for you to appreciate the possibilities.'

Brand nodded, his keen brain dissecting this information. In a world increasingly dependent on high-speed communications, Colman's space-relay system would have immense commercial value, quite apart from any other military use that might be made of it.

The professor went on: 'Of course, the complete set-up with three stations must necessarily come later. Our immediate plan is to get one satellite into orbit, linking this country — and Europe — directly with the United States. In fact, it should be up there at this moment . . . '

'But it came back with Bourne,' Brand said. 'Automatically. And Weller removed the relay and handed it over to you. Right?'

'Right! Now we have to wait for another rocket to be prepared for launching. That will take . . . um . . . ' Colman tugged at his beard, ' . . . perhaps a fortnight.'

A fortnight. Two weeks. Brand's mind raced. He had a feeling that things would be coming to a head long before that time. This was one case he had to wrap up in a hurry.

'I'd like to see the equipment that came back with Peter Bourne,' he said.

Colman frowned, but unlocked a safe. Brand crossed the laboratory. It was an ordinary steel safe with a double-acting tumbler lock. A cracksman would take no more than a minute to open it.

The professor reached inside the safe and lifted out a metal cylinder about nine inches long and some three inches in diameter. He unscrewed one end of the cylinder and slid out what appeared to be a solid, plastic block.

The plastic was transparent and Blake saw, embedded in it, a battery of what looked like tiny crystals. It was a marvel of precision electronic engineering.

'This,' said Professor Colman proudly, 'is my invention. It is the relay I told you about. My 'communicator.' It is the culmination of years of research, and the reason for this station's very existence. It is an automatic electronic repeater capable of doing everything that I have described to you. All that and, in fact, very much more.

'It receives, amplifies and transmits — on low power at that. It can handle millions of signals simultaneously. Its importance and unique nature lies not so much in what it is capable of — though this, even if I do say so myself, is fantastic enough. But, no, its true importance lies in its small size and exceptionally light weight. It is this extraordinary compactness which makes it possible to place a relay of this exceedingly complex nature in orbit with relatively small rockets and their limited pay-loads.'

Brand said sharply: 'Is this the only

relay of its kind in existence, professor?'

Colman returned his invention to the safe, relocked the door, and dropped the key into his pocket. 'No, but it *is* the only one with such vast capacity. It will completely revolutionise telecommunications.'

He said: 'There is only one such 'communicator'. These instruments aren't built in five minutes. We have tested this one exhaustively, of course, as far as we are able to simulate spatial conditions in this laboratory. And it functions perfectly. We are, however, waiting to test it in actual operation in space before going ahead with the manufacture of the other two 'communicators' that we will require for our programme.'

'And where do you keep your blue-prints?' Brand wanted to know.

Colman tapped his forehead. 'In here,' he said briefly.

Brand wondered about the professor. There could be no doubt of his technical brilliance — but did he fully realise the danger that threatened him?

Abruptly, the detective asked: 'Why was

Bourne's rocket fitted with manual control?'

'The communicator it carried was lodged in a satellite which was to be positioned *precisely* in outer space. We could not rely on automatic machinery and remote control in case something unexpected happened. A human is always to be preferred to robotics in an emergency, because he can improvise. It follows that the pilot of the rocket had to have control over his craft.'

Now it was Brand's turn to pace the floor, analysing the information which had been presented to him. One thing seemed to stand out very clearly. Peter Bourne had been killed to ensure the return of the communicator. But why had Weller been shot?

As he wrestled with the problem, he heard Colman snort.

'This Security business makes me laugh!' the professor said. 'I'm a scientist. This is my job and, as long as I'm allowed to get on with it, I don't much care who runs the show. Why should I? Does it really matter?'

'It might,' Brand answered carefully, 'in certain circumstances.'

'Politicians are fools, Mr. Brand. They can't see beyond the tips of their own smelly noses. All this fuss . . . but do you think they can see the end result? Of course they can't!'

The professor jabbed the air with his cheroot.

'Imagine the world in a few years' time . . . when anyone can speak direct to any part of the globe for a fraction of the present cost, when worldwide radio and television broadcasts are commonplace . . . internal censorship will be as dead as the Dodo! And *that* isn't going to please some people . . . '

As Simon Brand left the laboratory, he already seemed to hear the voice of the satellite. And it whispered of big money, military advantage, political power — and sudden death.

★   ★   ★

Marla had already told her story. Now Nick was on the line. Brand sat alone in

Bob Frost's office, behind the door labelled 'Security.' He spoke tersely into the phone.

'Break out the guns, Nick, and bring my Luger up to the station. From this moment, we all go armed.'

'Okay, chief.'

'As regards the other matters you raised — I'll do some checking on Marilyn Martin myself. And on Vogel. And also on this character Rushton who interests Vogel so much.'

'Fair enough, chief.'

'But,' Brand said, 'there is something else you can do. I want you to pick up two portable transistor radio sets in Oakhampton. The smaller the better. And I want an electric soldering iron, and a quantity of resin-cored solder.'

Nick said, startled, 'What on earth . . . '

Brand's voice was brittle. 'Just get them, Nick.' And he put the phone back.

Seconds later, he was dialling again.

This time, he put through a call to London. At length, a dry old voice announced without preamble: 'Kaner.'

'Brand. I want a check run on a Miss

Marilyn Martin. That may be only a professional name. She's a photographic model, and — ' he turned over Bob Frost's pin-up calendar and read the small print on the back. 'She posed for the Candid Glamour Calendar Company, this year's edition. I'd like a report on her background, known activities, contacts, and antecedents, and the name of the man who brought her down to Oakhampton.'

Kaner coughed. When he spoke again, his old voice held a note of urgency.

'Will do, Brand, but you've got to move fast! The pressure's on. I told you that American rockets were being used for this venture. Well, it's been suggested that their security forces take over. I want this business cleared up before the second rocket's due to be launched.'

There was a sharp click as the connection was broken. Again, Brand's finger dialled. He was busy, working against time, and he badly needed more information.

This time he had to wait longer to say what he really wanted to say. His voice now expressed sympathy, a reluctance to intrude on family grief. His questions were carefully phrased to avoid giving offence, for he was speaking to Peter Bourne's father.

'Yes . . . yes, I understand, Mr. Brand . . . ' The voice of Peter Bourne's father sounded hollow, drained of emotion. 'It's true that Peter was talking of starting out on a new career. He wasn't completely happy in the Service. He wanted to enter the world of business, and I believe he had a useful contact . . . a man called Rushton.'

A thoughtful frown creased Brand's brow as he replaced the telephone. Rushton . . .

He sat deep in thought behind Foster's desk until the bulky figure of Doctor Fenwick loomed in the doorway.

'You'll want this.' Fenwick opened a fat hand to reveal a raggedly-flattened high-velocity bullet. 'It's what killed Ben Weller.'

The ruddy-faced doctor sighed suddenly, and shook his head.

'You know, I used to think this place was dull. But not, any more. It's become a bit too damned lively, if you ask me. I'm only hoping it won't get any livelier.'

'Not if I can help it,' Brand returned evenly, and the doctor shook his head again, wonderingly. 'I ask you . . . two killings in twenty-four hours . . . '

Brand eyed him thoughtfully.

'Tell me, doctor,' he said. 'About Peter Bourne . . . you passed him as fit. Was he likely to have imagined two previous attempts on his life?'

Fenwick looked startled.

'Not Bourne! He was the cool, calculating type. No imagination at all. But just perfect for piloting an aircraft or manning a rocket.'

The door opened again, and Frost, the security chief, walked in wearily. Fenwick waved a casual hand. 'Be seeing you.' He went out.

'No trace,' Frost said heavily to Brand. 'My men are still out on the Moor, but the killer's away by this time.' He slumped into a chair. 'You know something . . . ? This makes a second murder revolving around Melanie Bourne.'

Brand raised an eyebrow. Then: 'Tell

me about the earlier attempts on Bourne's life,' he suggested. 'He reported them to you?'

'Yes . . . ' Frost admitted it reluctantly. 'I thought he was imagining things. Both could have been accidental. The first was a near-miss by a car. The second the result of an electrical fault.'

'Hmm . . . ' Brand pondered this answer. Then he said, 'Do you know anybody called Rushton?'

'Of course.' Frost stroked his moustache. 'Len Rushton . . . representing the small American financial interest in what we're doing here. You'll find him in the Admin. block.'

'Thanks.' Brand rose briskly. 'I'll see him now.'

He crossed the concrete compound to a block of offices; inquired at the reception desk.

'Yes, sir. This way, please. Mr. Rushton is expecting you . . . '

The office was large and airy.

Len Rushton, wearing a red-and-white check shirt and olive gaberdine slacks, held out a big paw; his sleeves were rolled up to show hairy arms.

'You've got results to report, Brand?' His manner was curt. 'I'm telling you, if it hadn't been for your reputation I'd have insisted on the F.B.I. being brought in by now. Two murders at a time like this! Do you realise that the consortium of American interests I represent has millions of bucks staked on this deal? It makes me sweat just to think about it!'

Brand's face showed some surprise. 'But I understood that the American financial interest in what's happening here was rather small.'

'Small it may be, in relation to all the other — mainly European — money involved,' Rushton said sourly. 'But it still runs to millions of bucks, and I'd hate like hell to see it go down the drain. And my principals would hate it, too, Brand. So much so — ' he added grimly. ' — that it's not going to happen!'

He continued tautly, 'I'll still call in the F.B.I. if necessary — and to hell with how your Security boys feel about it. They're American rockets you're using — whether you know it or not. In the last analysis, your people will have to play ball with us — or else. I tell you, Brand, I want results!'

'I'm pursuing several lines of inquiry,' Brand said quietly, 'and I think you can help me.'

'Me . . . ? Okay, if you say so. Shoot your questions.'

'Peter Bourne wanted a job with you. Is that right?'

'Oh, sure. But he was no good to me. Money-wise, he was just a mere babe in arms. A fine pilot, though. I turned him down flat. I told him to stick to what he knew.'

Brand digested this.

Then he said, 'Does the name Vogel mean anything to you? I've heard he's in Oakhampton, looking for you.'

Rushton scowled.

'I'll say it means something! The consortium I represent is made up of big American telecommunications interests — '

'And Vogel?' Brand inquired.

'He has interests in American tv and radio, too. But he's outside the consortium. And right from the beginning, he wanted in. And he's a hard man to throw, Brand. Real mean. He wants a share of the profits coming our way, and he's making like he means to get them. He'll never stop trying. But it's no deal, Brand. You understand — ?'

Rushton's voice had risen.

'It's no deal at all, Brand. You get that? If you see him, tell him, from me — it's no deal!'

# 6

## The watching eye

The night was inkily black on the Moor. Cloud obscured the faint starlight, and the moon had yet to rise.

Brand crouched motionless, head to one side, listening to the sound of the wind, the distant hoot of a hunting owl and the soft pad-pad of some small animal through the heather.

The weight of the Luger, snug under his armpit, comforted him.

He moved on slowly, circuitously clinging to cover, careful at all times never to silhouette himself against the distant floodlights of the research station. He made no sound, and left few traces as he inched his way towards the clump of bushes he had investigated earlier.

The Moor late at night was an eerie place with a life of its own. Long grass rustled. The wind moaned round the high granite tors. A nesting bird suddenly took wing. But it was none of these things that Brand was listening for.

He was after a killer. A cunning killer. A vanishing man.

He kept a tight hold on his nerves as he advanced. He felt the ground rise gently beneath him, then sink away again. He heard the tinkle of water not far away. Then he reached the clump of bushes. It was from here that the chief technician, Ben Weller, had been shot. Brand was sure of it.

Again he crouched motionless, senses tuned to capture the slightest sound.

Nothing stirred beyond the normal night life of the Moor. Nothing alarmed its denizens.

Silently, he wriggled deeper into cover. Lying prone on the bare earth, a bower of greenish-brown leaves hid him completely from view. He settled down to wait. Presently, just before midnight, the moon would rise, and from this vantage point he would certainly be able to see without himself being seen. He needed and possessed, infinite patience.

A wild wind keened over the land, but Brand made no movement. The night air chilled him. Insects crawled over him . . .

And time passed.

Then the moon swam smoothly through cloud, casting a thin, silver light over rock and bracken, and Brand produced a pair of minute but exceedingly powerful binoculars. Methodically, he began to range over the ground all around him. He subjected every stone, every bush, every tussock of heather to a searching scrutiny. And then, suddenly, he tensed.

He had seen something.

Had he been standing upright, he almost certainly would not have seen it: a minute glitter of glass in the moonlight. To his angle of vision, standing erect, there would have been no glitter at all.

But he was not standing erect. He was sprawled on the ground. And the glittering object was at this level.

Simon Brand frowned.

It was about thirty yards away from him, in the centre of a clump of gorse bushes. Eyes narrowed intently, Brand slowly moved his head from side to side. Now he could determine that the glittering object was circular, of about two inches diameter, and that it was moving, too.

Its movement was through a slow arc, on an axis. It turned one way through an angle of forty-five degrees, paused, then crept back. Brand's first thought was that what he could see was the lens of a telescope or monocular being used by some other hidden observer, scanning the ground. But then he had second thoughts — rapidly.

Try as he might, he could pick out no shadowy shape behind the glitter of glass and, in any case, the movements of the mysterious object were far too precise and regular to be directly controlled by any human hand.

What was it, then? What was he looking at? What could he see?

There was only one way to find out.

With infinite care, Brand inched himself forward on a slow, stealthy circuit. And, arriving behind the glittering object deep in the clump of gorse bushes, he saw that his careful approach had been amply justified.

What he saw staggered him.

He was looking at a rectangular metal box about twelve inches long by nine inches deep by six inches wide. He watched it slowly turn through an arc, and then track back again.

Just one look at it told him what it was.

Lenses jutted out of it, covering the ground all the way to the research station. Cables snaked away from it to a short whip aerial screened from view by the spikes of gorse.

Brand dragged in a breath.

What he was looking at was an all-seeing eye: a tireless spy for somebody, somewhere.

What he was looking at was a battery-operated television camera, ceaselessly keeping the research station under surveillance!

★　★　★

On another part of the Moor, at about the same time as Simon Brand was making his staggering discovery, Melanie Bourne was walking alone.

There was emptiness in her, an emptiness of the heart. Peter, her beloved Peter, was dead.

She walked mechanically, seeking in the still night a balm for her pain. A restlessness tormented her. At first, she could not believe that Peter would never come back to her. Acceptance had followed, and bitter tears. Then emptiness: a void of emotion slowly being filled by another, a different need. A need for revenge.

Peter had been deliberately murdered, and she speculated on the person who had killed him. As yet, she had no idea of the murderer's identity, nor of a motive. But hatred of the person who had killed him burned hotly inside her. She would find him and kill him with her own hands.

The moon showed through a break in the cloud. She was not aware how far she had walked: was only vaguely conscious of her direction. Nothing mattered now but revenge.

Her beautiful face took on an expression of grim and savage determination. Nothing was going to stop her. Nothing!

Ben Weller had died, too. That was strange . . . and somehow related to the death of her husband. She felt confused because none of it made sense. She knew that Peter and Weller had both been engaged on secret work. Perhaps in that fact lay a motive. She would have to learn the secret they had shared . . .

Thinking in this fashion, she paused and seemed to look around her.

But, in fact, she didn't see her surroundings at all. She was indifferent to them. She was intent on her thoughts.

So inwardly intent was she that she remained totally unaware of the fact that she had hesitated within a few yards of a copper rod that poked vertically out of a mound of huge boulders. Her unseeing eyes wandered over the rod, and still its existence did not register on her.

But her close proximity to the rod — a receiving aerial for low-powered television signals from Brand's part of the Moor — certainly registered on somebody else.

That someone was a man. A big man, in a cave in the rocks, who took one look at the disturbed and distorted picture on the televiewer in front of him, and grabbed up a gun with an oath.

It was the gun that had shot down Ben Weller. The man took it out of the cave at a shambling run. Someone was snooping around outside — this he knew. And snoopers could be very dangerous. Melanie Bourne would never know, never dream, how close she came to death in the minute that followed. The man with the gun scrambled out into the open. But, luckily for Melanie Bourne, she had moved on — away from the mound of huge boulders, and away from the aerial rod. And, also luckily for her, the moon chose that moment to scud behind cloud. The man with the gun caught only one glimpse of her; enough for identification purposes later, but no use for any other purposes now.

Unwillingly, reluctantly, he took his gun away from his shoulder. Of course, he could have gone after Melanie Bourne and probably caught up with her, but to have done so would have been to have flagrantly disobeyed orders. His instructions were to stay close to the televiewer, maintaining a constant watch on the research station, and await further orders over the two-way radio link also set up in the cave. He didn't disobey orders because he didn't dare disobey them.

He went back to the cave and the two-way radio link, and reported what had happened. He told his boss, whom he feared, what he had seen. Meanwhile, in his own part of the Moor, Simon Brand was examining the television camera that he had discovered. He was examining it without actually touching it or getting in front of its roving lens. But, nevertheless, he rapidly reached certain conclusions.

To begin with — the murder of Weller and, presumably, the killing of Peter Bourne, too, could not be considered merely as unhappy incidents in isolation. This Brand had already suspected. Now he had proof. They weren't just haphazard happenings.

One or both murders — certainly

Weller's — was plainly an integral part of some plan.

The totally unexpected discovery of a televisor here on Dartmoor made this inescapable. There was an organisation at work here: an alien organisation responsible for Ben Weller's death and, possibly, for Peter Bourne's, too. So much was sure.

No individual could, or would, employ equipment of the calibre he had discovered.

But this was only one of the conclusions Brand reached, and there were others.

The televisor was battery operated, which meant — perforce — that the signals it transmitted were effective only over a very limited area. Brand put the maximum range of the equipment at not more than five miles.

And this in turn meant that within a circle of this approximate radius there was some kind of outpost of the organisation that had killed Weller as a part of its greater plans.

Where, precisely, could that outpost be? Brand couldn't even begin to guess. A circle of the radius he postulated covered an area of close on eighty square miles. That was a lot of moor! But one thing Brand did know. He knew a simple way of locating the outpost.

In daylight, he would return to the Moor and look for tracks to and from the televisor. These must surely exist — however slight. Someone must have put the equipment in its present position, and someone — presumably based on the outpost the televisor fed with its signals — must service it and change the batteries that powered it.

Now Brand moved.

Cautiously, he eased himself away from the televisor and worked through a circuitous route back to the research station. What he had discovered gave him food for thought, and a reason for action later.

For the moment, he was content to wait.

An alien organisation was at work here. He had proof of that. And all organisations have leaders.

He was content to wait until he had the means of unmasking the key man behind the killers on the Moor.

# 7

## Playing with fire

Some minutes after midnight, powdered and perfumed and fresh from a hot bath, Marilyn Martin sat in front of her dressing table. She wore a filmy flower-patterned housecoat of Chinese style, insecurely fastened, and as she brushed her flame-coloured hair she practised her most seductive smile on the mirror.

Something had gone wrong. By now they should have been away, the whole thing settled. Her face lost its artificial smile and developed a scowl; hastily, she eased her features back into a professional mould. Tonight, she had to please someone . . . a lot depended on her.

There was a strong element of risk, which was why they had first decided on the other plan. But that had gone wrong. Now it was up to her.

She varnished her nails and breathed

on them. She painted her mouth bright red. She rose to make one final inspection of her room in the *Wheat Sheaf.* Everything was ready; the low couch, the subdued lighting, the whisky bottle, the glasses . . .

There came a faint tap on the door. Even now her caller sounded uncertain of her, or of himself. It was as well, she thought. He'd be easier to handle.

She crossed the room, composed her voice. 'Yes? Who is it?'

'It's me, darling.' His voice was a low, furtive mutter. 'It's me. Bob.'

She unlocked the door, and Bob Frost slid swiftly and secretively inside. She closed the door and snapped down the catch.

'Bob, dear . . . '

She flung her arms round his neck and kissed him with simulated passion, pressing her body hard against his. She felt him respond to the lure.

As she broke away, his eye followed her faithfully. The Chinese housecoat sagged open and he caught a glimpse of lavender-tinted underwear and of slender limbs clothed in black nylon mesh stockings.

She covered herself slowly, smiling a painted smile. This was going to be easy . . . Bob Frost, Chief Security Officer at Intercontinental Communications, was in his forties. A bachelor. And lonely. Love seemed to have passed him by and now, approaching middle-age, desperation blinded him to the kind of woman Marilyn Martin was. Frost was infatuated.

'Marilyn, you look lovely,' he muttered, almost stammering like a schoolboy.

She poured the whisky and handed him a glass, smiling slowly. She brushed against him tantalisingly. 'It's nice to be appreciated, darling.'

He drained his whisky at a gulp and she refilled his glass, leading him to a deep armchair. She slid smoothly, with practised competence, into his lap, and mussed his hair with assumed affection.

'You haven't been to see me for two whole days,' she complained. 'I was getting lonesome . . . feeling neglected.'

'It's been difficult,' Frost mumbled. 'I have to be careful.'

Rita Randall smiled to herself. She had to be careful, too, playing around with two men at near enough the same time. But she enjoyed playing with them.

Frost's clammy hand rested on her nyloned knee. His fingers trembled. 'Wouldn't it be wonderful, Bob,' she murmured into his ear, 'if you didn't have to be careful ever again? Can't you picture it . . . ? Just the two of us, together, lying on a sun-drenched beach somewhere in the south of France . . . '

'Marilyn . . . if only we could!' His lips nuzzled her throat. His hands, restless, drew her closer.

'But, of course, we could, darling,' she whispered, 'if you'd do one small favour for a friend of mine. He's a very rich friend. I'm sure he'd pay well. Enough to make our plans come true.'

Reluctantly taking one hand away from her for a moment, he picked up his glass and finished his whisky. Casually, she refilled the glass.

'It's so simple, darling. Really it is. She chose her words with care. 'This friend of mine wants to meet somebody on the station. Somebody called — Rush? No, that's not right. Rushton? Yes, that's it! Rushton! I expect you know him. He's some kind of financial contact-man, apparently. Anyway, it's nothing to do with your silly security nonsense, so you don't have to worry.'

She snuggled closer, warm and scented, eager to please.

Bob Frost found himself trembling uncontrollably.

Marilyn Martin said: 'My friend just wants to talk to Rushton, but it seems he's too busy to leave the station. And my friend hasn't much time. All you have to do is make out a pass for him . . . a pass to get him into the station.'

'I can't do it — '

'Of course you can, Bob, darling!' She nibbled his ear. 'I wouldn't ask you to do anything wrong. It's just something to do with a business deal, some financial killing, nothing to worry about. And then we'll have lots of money to go abroad and laze in the sun together.'

She gave a long sigh and stretched one slim, black nylon clad leg in front of him.

'So don't be stuffy, darling. Just give me the pass, and — '

'I can't!'

Marilyn saw beads of sweat gathered along Frost's ragged moustache. His pale brown eyes were glazed over. His voice lacked firmness. He'd do it all right. She'd just have to play him a little longer, like a fish on a line.

She refilled his glass once more. 'Just for me . . . ' she murmured in his ear. 'Do it just for me . . . '

'No, Marilyn.' His voice was an unwilling mumble. 'I have a position of trust — there are secrets — '

'You and your secrets, Bob! Really, sometimes I think you're not human.'

Casually, she got up and moved across the room, moving into the shadows. Her lips parted invitingly as Frost got to his feet unsteadily, and came after her.

The back of her legs nudged the edge of the couch.

He reached for her avidly. His trembling hands tried to fasten on her in a kind of sick desperation.

But she held him off.

'Bob,' she said softly, 'you will help my friend, won't you . . . ?'

She heard his answer.

And, some moments later, she reached up from the couch and turned off the light.

★   ★   ★

Forty-five minutes later, Nick gripped Marla Dean's arm and drew her quickly back round a bend in the hotel corridor.

It was one o'clock in the morning: hardly the time to be caught soft-footing around.

But Nick had seen Marilyn Martin's midnight visitor arrive with exaggerated caution and stealth and had been consumed with curiosity. He had recognised the man instantly from the gallery of photographs of all the research station's staff with which Kaner had supplied Brand at the outset of this investigation.

What was Frost up to? The obvious — or . . . ?

Nick still didn't know. And now Frost was leaving.

From around the bend in the hotel corridor, Nick and Marla watched him go. Marla with eyebrows raised. 'Well . . . '

No doubt in *her* mind, Nick thought, as to why Frost had crept so stealthily into the hotel at dead of night.

Why, he wondered, did women invariably think the worst of a man? And they did. Give them any situation and they'd soon reduce it to its lowest common denominator. And, brother, that was low!

Mind you, and here Nick's memory gave him a sly nudge, they were probably usually right . . .

But there such a reflection came to an abrupt end for Nick. For no sooner had Frost crept down the stairs and away than Marilyn Martin's door was stealthily opening again. This time, it was Marilyn herself who slipped out. She was dressed for the street, and she hesitated at the stairhead listening intently, clearly concerned that Frost should be well out of the way before she left the hotel herself.

Where was she going at this time of night?

Nick thought that question might have

an interesting answer.

Plainly Marla Dean thought so, too, for as soon as Marilyn Martin started to move down the stairs Marla was moving as well — after her

'Hey — wait a minute!' Nick protested in an urgent whisper.

'Wait nothing!' said Marla, equally urgently. 'You've got a key to that room. She gave you one. Why, I hate to imagine. But now here's your chance. Use it. Use the key. I'll keep an eye on her.'

'But — '

But it was no use. Marla had swiftly and silently sped out of earshot.

Nick sighed.

If Marilyn drove off somewhere in a car, how could Marla follow her? For himself, he'd have had no qualms about borrowing a vehicle from the hotel forecourt. No one would know.

But would Marla think of that . . . ?

In fact, Marla already had.

She had arrived out in front of the hotel just in time to see Marilyn Martin driving off in a blue Ford Escort.

Well, no one would know, she told

herself as she darted down a long line of cars parked in the forecourt, trying doors, trying to wrestle one open.

No one would know if she borrowed a car for an hour or so to trail Marilyn.

A door was unlocked, midway down the line. The car was a Ford Mondeo.

Even as she ripped wires out from under the dashboard to short out the ignition and get the car started, Marla was telling herself that the wires could be put back as she'd found them, no difficulty there; Nick could do it; and certainly no one would know.

Unhappily, both she and Nick — secure in this belief — could not have been more wrong.

★  ★  ★

Marla moved fast. She drove the Mondeo flat out to catch up with Marilyn. She wanted to know where the other girl was going, and why. Marilyn Martin turned left by the Town Hall, taking the road to the Moor. Marla's interest quickened.

As the town dropped away behind,

Marilyn Martin increased her speed. The blue Escort flashed away, and Marla's foot came down hard on the accelerator.

A mile further on, the Escort left the road and took to a rough track heading across the Moor. Gravel sprayed from beneath the spinning wheels of the Mondeo as Paula concentrated on keeping the other car in sight. Stunted trees flashed past. A wild, desolate stretch of yellow-brown bracken showed up in the headlights. Marilyn Martin was not heading for the research station, Marla thought, nor was she reducing speed even though the track degenerated with every passing mile.

By now, Marilyn Martin must be aware that she was being followed. There were only the two cars on this part of the Moor. Marla's Mondeo would be fast-moving headlights in the other girl's rear-view mirror.

The track twisted and turned. In some places it consisted only of jagged flints pounded down by passing carts. It was no surface for fast driving, but the redheaded Marilyn did not slacken speed. Brow furrowed, Marla gripped the wheel of the Mondeo, intent on holding her own.

Stones beat a tattoo under the mudguards. Flying gravel lashed the paintwork. A puncture at this speed could prove fatal, yet Marla kept her foot hard down. She was committed to this chase now, and there was no going back.

The track snaked across empty Devonian moorland between outcrops of rock. Then Marla saw a hairpin bend ahead and, beyond, a rough stone bridge, high and humpbacked. What lay on the other side?

Marilyn Martin took the hairpin bend at speed. Marla eased back a fraction. Marilyn Martin was in the first bend, out of sight. The high stone bridge blocked Marla's view as she roared into the hairpin. She swung the wheel, aiming for the centre of the bridge . . . and saw with horror that the blue Ford Escort was parked across the road dead in her path.

Tyres shrieked a protest as she braked to avoid collision. She fought the skid as massive grey stonework loomed ominously nearer with every second.

And then she heard a sound that chilled her blood . . . the vicious stammer of machine-gun fire.

In that moment, Marla Dean knew she had been lured into a trap from which there was no way out. From the corner of her eye she glimpsed a figure in the gorse handling a submachine-gun.

Then a tyre burst.

The Mondeo slewed.

And a hail of bullets slammed into the bodywork, riddling the car like a sieve.

# 8

## A house in the country

It was two o'clock in the morning, and Boris Josef Vogel was in residence.

The house was old and built to last, set in its own grounds. It lay south of Oakhampton, just off the main road.

Vogel had been hesitant about coming here tonight because the house had been empty for four years before he had bought it, and there had been some doubt as to whether it would be ready — completely refurbished — in time to receive him.

He need not have worried.

Relays of charwomen had swept and polished; pantechnicons had delivered luxury suites; the essential services had been speedily reconnected and a giant-size refrigerator installed. With money no object, everyone had worked quickly.

Now the house was a place fit for a

king . . . or Boris Josef Vogel.

High financier, cartel king, manipulator of men's lives, Vogel had arrived in the district to take over the reins of his local enterprise in person. He was tired of underlings who bungled every move that he planned. From now on, he promised himself grimly, there would be no more mistakes.

The night was dark and a mist rolled in from the Moor to blanket the old house. Inside, light blazed behind heavy curtains. Deep armchairs settled into luxuriously thick carpets. The retinue of City-suited hatchet-men and starlets sat silent: hard eyes ceaselessly watching doors and windows; painted mouths sipping gin-slings.

Boris Vogel clasped a glass of brandy and benedictine and brooded. Lines grooved his bald skull. No one in the room made the slightest sound while he concentrated.

Then a doorbell pealed distantly into the silence. One of the slim-shouldered, unsmiling men hefted a gun in his hand and paced out of the room. He returned with a second man, dressed in grey and powerfully built.

It was the man who, only a few hours earlier, had come within a hair's breadth of taking Melanie Bourne's life.

'About time, Hurley,' Vogel greeted him coldly. 'You took long enough getting here.'

Hurley was a big man, and he looked competent. Normally, he was very sure of himself. But, facing Vogel, he appeared uncertain.

He moved awkwardly, and said placatingly, 'I had quite a way to come, Vogel. I set out as soon as I got the message.'

'I suppose we'll just have to be thankful for that,' Vogel growled. He held out his glass and one of the starlets promptly refilled it. He said abruptly: 'You found someone snooping around?'

'Yes.' Hurley described Melanie Bourne. And Vogel listened grimly.

Then he said: 'Know who she was?'

'No, Mr. Vogel. That is . . . not for certain. She looked like Bourne's wife. But in that light I couldn't be absolutely sure.'

'Make sure.' It was an order. 'Then take

care of her. I'm not having anything else going wrong. Is that understood? There's too damn much gone wrong around here!'

Hurley said uneasily: 'It's not our fault, Mr. Vogel. Things just happened. How were we to know? I mean — this job's been hard enough to fix without someone on the inside. You can't read minds through a televisor.'

The voice of Boris Vogel hardened into something virulently mean and incredibly vicious. 'Excuses! Excuses! All I seem to get these days are excuses. I want results! You hear me? And by God I mean to have them! As for that man Rushton — I'd certainly like to lay my hands on him. And I will! I'll make him wish he'd never been born!'

Vogel was ablaze with fury.

A tense silence developed in the room. Hurley eyed the venomous, bald and grossly corpulent figure in front of him with obvious uncertainty. Then he said slowly, 'Is there time for that, Mr. Vogel?'

The other man glared at him. 'What do you mean?'

Hurley shrugged. 'This fellow Brand is

pretty good. He's been sent down here from London. He's at the research station asking one hell of a lot of questions and poking around. He might come up with some answers soon.'

Vogel sneered thickly 'You terrify me!'

He said: 'I've heard all about Brand. Agreed, he has a reputation. But — ' he bit the words off ' — I'll fix him, too, never fear.'

Hurley said doubtfully. 'It would be better to leave him alone, Mr. Vogel. Brand is a bad man to tangle with. Some very tough men have come to grief trying to fix him. It would be better to move fast, to my way of thinking. Forget Brand, forget Rushton. Just get the job done. Get it over.'

Vogel growled: 'We'll do this my way, Hurley.'

'I still think — '

'Shut up!' Vogel snarled furiously. 'I'm doing the thinking from now on. There've been enough mistakes!'

Hurley relapsed into silence.

Vogel sipped his brandy and benedictine and dreamed a little. He thought about Simon Brand's secretary, the beautiful blonde Marla Dean. She obviously hadn't realised when they had encountered each other that he had known very well who she was.

Hurley, awaiting orders, let his gaze rest on the two starlets. It would be nice, he thought, to have either one of them down in the cave with him. It would certainly relieve the awful boredom . . .

Looking more closely at the brunette, he remembered seeing her in an adult-rated horror film a year or so before. She'd suffered a terrible fate in the very first reel. Her performance, Hurley remembered, had been equally terrible.

Abruptly, Vogel spoke. 'We're making one quick grab. Straight in, pick up the communicator, out. You'll be told when. Soon. Maybe tomorrow night. Be ready.'

It was dismissal. Hurley grunted, 'Right, Mr. Vogel,' and went from the room, out of the big house into the thickening mist and back across the Moor.

Vogel set down his empty glass and yawned. The City-suited hatchet-men accurately recognised their cue and faded out of the room.

A gold watch ticked loudly into another silence. The two starlets came alert as deep-set eyes in an inscrutable face contemplated their charms. The perky blonde. The sultry brunette. Vogel deliberated over them.

He remembered that Brand's remarkable secretary was a blonde.

He sent the brunette away with a few polite words of dismissal.

Now there were only the two of them in the room: the obese Vogel and the young blonde would-be actress.

The blonde, whose name was Lynn, had appeared in bit parts in several minor British pictures. After that, no one had taken up the option on her contract. She had been photographed at a few film premieres, been the rounds of casting directors, and had heard promises made and seen them broken. Eventually, somebody had introduced her to Mr. Vogel at a party. Now, at least she ate regularly.

Vogel reached for a set of push-buttons beside his chair. The room flooded with sound: music with an insistent beat. Lynn moved into the centre of the room. She began to sway to the music.

Seated in deep shadow beyond the penumbra of central light, Vogel refilled his glass and watched the blonde. His eyes were half closed.

His tongue licked at a salty drop of perspiration gathering above his upper lip. He leaned forward, hands clasping his knees, staring intently at the swaying girl.

The music quickened. It throbbed like an urgent pulse.

Then: 'That will do, girlie,' said Vogel, speaking thickly. 'Stop the music.'

And she obeyed.

★    ★    ★

Nick searched Marilyn Martin's room very thoroughly indeed.

He went through her wardrobe, the drawers of the dressing table, a travelling case. He looked behind the curtains, and stripped the bed. He investigated the couch.

There was a small notepad beside the telephone, and he held it up to the light. A faint impression showed where someone, presumably Marilyn herself, had written on the sheet above and torn it off. That page was now missing.

Nick carefully detached the indented top sheet; even faint impressions could be made to reveal their secrets with the right treatment.

He put everything in the room back as he'd found it, and took one last look round to satisfy himself that he'd overlooked nothing. He locked the door, and returned to his room.

There he opened his case and took out his photographic equipment. Clipping the indented sheet from the telephone pad to a flat board, he changed the bulb of his bedside lamp for one of higher power, and arranged the light so that it fell obliquely across the indented impressions. He adjusted the aperture and shutter speed of his camera.

He worked methodically. It was very late, and getting later, but this might be important . . . and oblique-illumination photography, besides revealing the words that had been scrawled on the pad would make a permanent record of them.

He focused and exposed, then blacked out the room and began a developing and printing routine. When he had finished he had a copy of the number that had been written on the missing top sheet of the telephone pad.

Seeing the number written out threw him out of his stride for a moment, but only a moment. It must be a telephone number. And in all probability the number of the man who gave Marilyn Martin her orders. What else could it be?

What else . . . ? An inner voice — dented Nick's confidence. It could be the number of the butcher, the baker, or the candlestick-maker.

All right, Nick told the inner voice.

Laugh all you want to. But there's a very quick way to find out who's right isn't there?

He lifted the bedside telephone.

There was a moment's pause, the burr-burr of ringing tone, then a clipped, business-like voice: 'Mr. Vogel's residence. Who's calling?'

Thoughtfully, Nick replaced the receiver.

# 9

## The intruder

Marla knew a moment of terror. She was charging the bridge at high speed, the blue Ford Escort dead in her path. And bullets ricochetted around her.

It was the burst tyre that saved her life. The Mondeo slewed round, spoiling the killer's aim. And as the car struck the stonework of the bridge, Marla got a door open. She was hurled out and down.

She arced through fifteen feet of air. She hit water and sprawled, stunned, in the shallow stream under the bridge. Blood flowed from a gash on her forehead. She gasped for air; then froze as she heard a movement on the bridge above her.

Someone was leaning over and peering down through the darkness.

'It's a woman!' A man's voice was sharp with surprise. Then it set hard in suspicion. 'I thought you radioed it was a man following you, Marilyn. I thought you said it must be Brand.'

Marilyn Martin's voice was high-pitched. 'So I made a mistake! But she was tailing me. You saw her yourself. And she's dead now. You've killed her! For God's sake let's get away from here!'

Marla remained motionless. Water swirled around her. The passing seconds seemed endless . . .

Then —

'Yeah . . . reckon you're right. She does look like a goner,' the man said callously. 'Who is she? Do you know?'

Marilyn Martin's voice was shrill. 'I can't see her properly from here, and I'm not going down! What are we wasting time for? Someone could have heard the crash. Someone could be along in a minute!'

'You're jumpy,' the man growled. 'Calm down!'

'I didn't bargain for murder!' Marilyn Martin was almost hysterical. 'You didn't have to kill her! I — '

'Shut up!' the man snarled, and there

was the pistol-shot sound of a savage slap. 'Shut up and calm down! What did you think we were going to do when you radioed through for help? Play a set of tennis with whoever was tailing you? Why don't you grow up!'

Marilyn Martin was sobbing.

'Aw, shut up!' the man growled. 'Shut up and come on!' And Marla heard receding footsteps, the sound of a car starting up and driving off. Only when silence returned, did she stir. She dragged herself to the bank, and wiped the blood from her face. She did her best to staunch the gash on her forehead. She felt utterly drained.

Presently, she climbed the bank to inspect the car she had been driving. It was a wreck: a job for a breakdown truck. She'd have to walk back to Oakhampton. She searched the gorse where the killer had been and found a lot of spent cartridge cases. But there was nothing to give her a clue as to the man's identity. Chilled to the bone, shivering violently, she set off on her long walk back to Oakhampton. Her head throbbed. With no hope of help, she forced the pace. The sooner she got back to the *Wheat Sheaf*, the better.

She considered leaving the track and cutting cross-country, and decided against it. It was misty. It would be very easy for her to lose her way. She had to stick to the track and keep moving.

She plodded forward, bruised muscles aching with every forced step. An hour dragged by. Then another. And another.

At four o'clock in the morning, she rang the night bell at the *Wheat Sheaf* in Oakhampton and hobbled into the hall under the stupefied stare of the hall porter.

'What on earth's been happening to you, miss?' the man got out.

'An accident . . . ' Marla mumbled, and that was all she could mumble. She was frozen to the marrow. And she felt exhausted.

But half an hour later, after a scalding-hot bath and steaming mug of coffee liberally laced with rum, she had recovered sufficiently to spill out her story to Nick, whom she had found, waiting somewhat anxiously, in her room.

And Nick wasted no time in informing Brand of what had been happening. Despite the late hour, he rang up his chief at the research station at once.

Brand was concerned. 'You're sure she's all right?'

'She's as right as rain — now. And the cut on her head isn't deep. I'll put her on the line, chief. She can tell you herself.'

And she did.

Then Brand heard Nick again.

'And I haven't been wasting my time, chief. There's no doubt about it, Marilyn Martin must be mixed up with Vogel. And this is why . . . '

Nick told Brand what he had discovered in the redhead's room, and what he had done about it.

He went on: 'After ringing the number, I checked with the telephone company and discovered that the number's a new one. It's only just been connected. And Vogel has only just moved into a big house he's bought outside Oakhampton . . . '

Brand heard his young partner out.

Then: 'Good work,' he commented. 'It

certainly does seem there's some connection between Marilyn Martin and Vogel. We appear to be getting somewhere, though we've still quite a way to go. After all, Vogel has only been down here a matter of hours, and that suggests that Marilyn Martin must have been taking orders from someone else, locally, before the big man himself arrived on the scene. I'd like to know who that 'someone' was. It could well be that the same person had a hand in Ben Weller's murder . . . '

He paused thoughtfully for a long moment, and then said: 'But we can go into all that in the morning. Meantime, tell Marla to get some sleep. Maybe you'd better give her a pill. And get some sleep yourself. I'll drop in at your place for breakfast, and we can go over everything then. And between now and then we'd better think what we're going to do about that crashed Mondeo, too.

'Obviously, the first thing is to find out who owns it. Equally obviously, compensation will have to be paid and some sort of explanation of what's happened to the car will have to be given to the owner.

Between now and breakfast you might spare a thought to what we can tell him.'

'Will do,' Nick said, and rang off. Gratefully, Brand made to return to his bed. But the phone rang again. Brand reached for it. Had Nick forgotten something?

He had not.

The detective said: 'Yes . . . ? Brand here.' And without preamble another voice answered him: 'Kaner.'

It was an old, dry voice rustling over the wire, and Brand immediately shook off his tiredness.

Kaner said: 'You asked about Marilyn Martin. She was well-known as a model about twelve months ago. Then she got mixed up with a private photographic club . . . one of the unsavoury kind . . . and disappeared when the police raided it. She hasn't been seen near her usual haunts since. But I do have a line on the man who's currently supposed to be keeping her. And when last seen he was in your part of the world.'

Brand was wide-awake now.

Could this be the 'someone' he'd been

discussing with Nick?

Kaner said: 'The man's name is Hurley . . . '

★ ★ ★

At that moment, Hurley himself was not far away from where Brand talked to Kaner over the telephone installed in the prefabricated bungalow on the research station that had been placed at the detective's disposal.

At that moment, Hurley was, in fact, getting out of a car that had halted before the main gates. He was approaching the guardhouse, a rugged featured, powerfully-built man dressed in a neat dark grey suit.

Ahead, light blazed in the guard house. It shone through an open door, illuminating the painted signboard that read: INTERCONTINENTAL COMMUNICATIONS. Immediately beyond the high wire fence was a pool of darkness, and beyond that a few scattered squares of light denoting office blocks and living quarters. The arc-lamps above the wire girdling the station had been extinguished. It was now nearly one o'clock in the morning.

But dawn was still some time away and, distantly, other high-powered lamps glared over the gantry where technicians were working all through the night to prepare the second rocket for launching.

Hurley approached the guardhouse with confident tread.

A uniformed security guard came out to meet him. 'Your pass, please, sir . . . ?'

Hurley showed a pass, and the guard inspected it carefully. But no more carefully than usual. He had not seen this man before, but that, in itself, was quite unremarkable. A lot of people the guard had never seen before had legitimate business at the station.

Nor was it remarkable that Hurley should have chosen to arrive at this early hour.

People with business at the station were constantly arriving and departing by night as well as by day. The guard saw that the Security pass was in order, bearing the official stamp and Bob Frost's signature.

'Your business, sir?'

Hurley said: 'I have to see Mr. Rushton urgently.'

The guard unlocked a side gate.

'You'll find Mr. Rushton's bungalow over there — beyond that big concrete building on your right.'

The guard returned to his post and logged the visitor. He'd seen the signature of Bob Frost, the Security Chief, often enough to recognise its genuineness. He didn't bother to call Rushton . . .

Hurley walked down the broad concrete road in the direction the guard had indicated. He hurried no more than any man would on urgent business. And Hurley's real business was very urgent indeed.

Only a few hours before, Mr. Vogel had intimated that there would be no attempt to steal Professor Colman's 'communicator' until the following night, at the earliest. But something had happened to alter all that. Marilyn Martin had been successful in obtaining a signed pass from Bob Frost, and Vogel had decided to waste no more time, but to strike at once.

Frost was a weak and wavering

character, and if the pass were to be used at all it were better that it was used quickly — before the Security Chief could have unfortunate second thoughts, or a dangerous change of mind.

So now, reaching a corner, Hurley slipped into shadow and edged his way over to the left. If his information was correct, he should be close to Professor Colman's laboratory.

He moved silently on thick, crepe soled shoes. His right hand was hard on the butt of the automatic in his pocket. He didn't anticipate trouble, but he wasn't going to be taken this side of the wire.

He paused to check his bearings, remembering every detail he had observed through the televisor. The workshops . . . the canteen . . . the power station. He advanced swiftly, sure of himself — only to check suddenly at the sound of approaching footsteps.

Rigid in a dark doorway into which he had darted, he waited for the chance contact to pass . . . and the shift-working technician never knew how near he was to death.

Then Hurley went on. He reached the long, low laboratory building. It was in darkness. He inserted a thin metal key into the lock and probed gently. The door opened, and he slid inside. For a moment he stood taut, motionless, listening.

Then he used a shielded torch. The light played over stools and benches. He heard the faint hum of air extractors, smelt the aroma of stale cigar smoke. He spotted the safe in the corner. Everything was just as it had been described to him. A smart girl, Marilyn, he thought. She'd got it right . . .

He contemplated the safe with a professional eye. Child's play. All that business with the wire, and security, and they kept the communicator in a tin box like this. His lip curled. Typically British, he thought. Amateurs! Again he used the thin metal key. Delicately, he felt for the tumblers, his hand steady as a rock. He didn't sweat even when he heard the final click.

The door of the safe swung open and he saw the cylinder, exactly as it had been described to him. His eyes glistened as he reached for it. This was it! The communicator! Carefully, he set the cylinder down on a bench and relocked the safe.

Then the beam of his torch flicked through the laboratory as he memorised the relative positions of benches and stools and the door. Carrying the cylinder, he moved confidently through the building. He reached the door and opened it and stepped outside, listening intently for any untoward sound. He heard nothing.

Carefully setting the cylinder down again, he relocked the door of the laboratory. If he left no obvious signs of robbery, it would not be discovered until Colman went to the safe in the normal course of events. Valuable time would be gained for the get-away.

Hurley didn't overlook a thing.

He hefted the cylinder under his arm, smiling a little. Someone was due for a shock. He kept in the shadows, working his way towards the wire.

A shadow-shape moved close at hand. Feet crunched on gravel. Hurley flattened himself against a wall, his automatic jutting menacingly. It would be just too bad if he were discovered now . . .

The cylinder was heavy beneath his arm. He crouched against the wall, waiting. The uniformed figure of a security guard passed on his round. It was lucky they didn't use dogs, Hurley thought. He waited until the man was well out of the way, and then moved swiftly.

He reached the wire at a prearranged point, and blinked his torch, once. On the far side of the fence, a man rose from the ground. No word was spoken.

Hurley took a firm grip on the cylinder, balanced it, then tossed it high in the air . . . over the wire.

The dark form waiting there grunted as he caught it, then turned smartly away and faded into the darkness shrouding the Moor.

* * *

Hurley turned back between silent buildings. His breath came easier now.

He was relaxed and confident as he

approached the Administration block.

He waited a moment, in shadow, studying the harshly lit road. There was no one to see him.

He stepped into the light and walked briskly towards the main gate, whistling softly. It had gone well. The cylinder was outside the wire and far away by now. It remained only to pass the guard on the gate.

He kept his hands out of his pockets.

He lit a cigarette as he showed his pass again. The guard had been changed: that, too, had been a part of the timing.

The new guard looked at Hurley carefully, then checked his log.

'Thank you, sir.'

Hurley rammed the pass back in his pocket and walked through the gate — unhurriedly — to where his car was waiting.

He gave no sign of the tremendous elation he felt. He had done it!

The secret of Professor Colman's communicator was in their hands at last.

# 10

## Consternation

Brand, Nick and Marla had finished breakfast; a substantial meal of grapefruit, bacon and eggs, toast, marmalade, and coffee. The dining room of the *Wheat Sheaf* was almost empty and Brand was leaning forward, talking seriously to his companions, when the waiter approached.

'Mr. Brand? You're wanted on the telephone, sir.' The detective stubbed out his cigarette and moved swiftly. He went out into the hall; picked up the phone.

The voice at the other end of the wire sounded urgent.

'Brand? You've got to get out here fast! Colman's communicator was stolen from his safe during the night!'

Brand sucked in a sharp breath.

Then: 'I'm on my way,' he said quickly, and rang off.

He returned briefly to the dining room. 'Nick, you're coming with me.'

Succinctly, he explained what had happened. 'Marla, arrange to have the Mondeo collected and repaired. As I told you earlier, I've settled everything with the owner.'

The breakfast party broke up.

And not many minutes later, Brand was braking his Bentley before Professor Colman's laboratory at the research station. He and Nick left the car quickly, and entered the building.

Three men waited for them. The professor paced the floor, puffing at a cheroot. He looked angry, and his voice rasped.

'Security! All this stupid security, and a common thief makes off with my work. I shall complain to the Minister. Heads will roll for this!'

In the background, Len Rushton scowled.

'I'm telling you, Brand you'd better get that communicator back — and quick! Millions of dollars are at stake. I'm bringing in American security to protect my interests in future. You limeys are worse than useless!'

Bob Frost, the Security Chief, said nothing. His eyes looked frightened.

'One at a time, please.' Brand raised a hand for silence. He stared across the laboratory at the iron safe. The door was open, and there was nothing inside the safe. Brand said: 'Tell me, professor, how did you discover that your communicator was missing?'

'I looked in the safe, of course,' Colman snapped. Then he checked himself. He grunted: 'Oh . . . I see what you mean.'

He said: 'The outer door of this laboratory was locked; everything appeared normal. The safe was locked, too. I had no suspicions. It was pure chance . . . I wanted to make a further test on the communicator. When I found the safe empty, I called Frost at once.'

Brand eyed the security man.

Frost licked his lips nervously. 'I checked with the guard on the gate. There was an early morning visitor logged to Mr. Rushton — '

'I never had a visitor,' Rushton growled. 'I keep telling you that I know nothing about it. That Security pass must have been a phoney, and the guard should have spotted it.'

Brand inspected the lock on the outer door of the laboratory and the lock on the safe. Neither showed any sign of being forced. The robbery had been a professional job. He glanced at Frost.

'Any idea how the communicator was taken out of this area?'

Frost looked miserable. 'I don't know yet. The man on the gate says he's absolutely certain that Rushton's visitor carried nothing out with him.'

Brand mused. 'Over the fence . . . '

'I've got men searching,' Bob Frost said shortly.

'What bothers me,' Brand said, is the Intelligence behind it. Someone knew exactly where to come. Nothing else at all has been touched. Just the communicator removed from the safe . . . '

He looked coldly at Frost.

'A normal security measure should have been for the guard on the gate to check with Mr. Rushton . . . and how did they get hold of a pass bearing your signature?'

Bob Frost said unhappily, 'I'll tighten up security all round.'

Rushton snorted. 'Guess you won't be around much longer after this, Frost. I'm sure getting some American boys in!'

'That won't be necessary.' Simon Brand pulled a wooden packing case from under one of the benches. He removed several great handfuls of shavings and, thrusting an arm deep into the box, pulled out a transparent plastic block studded with crystals.

'Here we are,' he said. And the others stared at him, astonished. Frost was the first to recover his voice.

'What is this, Brand? What are you playing at? Are you just trying to be clever at my expense?' The Security Chief was practically shouting. 'There's been no real robbery at all! It was a put-up job! A hoax! You arranged it! Why, you — you — '

Brand shook his head curtly. 'Nothing like that. I didn't think much of this safe, so I took what seemed to me to be a natural precaution. And it's just as well that I did. That burglary last night was no hoax. It was the real thing. And the thief would have got away with the real communicator, too, if I hadn't effected a small substitution. As it is, the thief got the communicator's container all right, but it was filled with an electronic gadget I wired up myself with parts cannibalised from two transistor radios. Round about now, someone should be getting 'Desert Island Discs' on the B.B.C. very loud and clear.'

'Whaal!' Rushton was laughing. He looked delighted. 'I guess you limeys aren't so dim after all! I take it all back! I'm telling you, Mr. Brand, that's one helluva weight off my mind!'

But the dapper, bearded professor looked angrier than ever before.

'You had no right to interfere without my permission!' he snapped at Brand. 'At the very least, you should have warned me! Why, you could easily have damaged my apparatus.'

'I handled it very carefully,' Brand returned quietly.

'That's not the point. Not the point at all!' Colman's cheroot showered ash as he waved an arm angrily. 'I should have been informed! In future, I insist that the communicator is not to be touched by anyone without my express permission. Is that clearly understood?'

Len Rushton grinned.

'In four days' time, professor, it'll be way out of reach of anyone wanting to touch it. Why, way out of reach! Out there — in space!'

'Four days — ?' Brand spoke sharply. 'What do you mean?'

Rushton turned. He said casually, 'I guess you haven't been told, Brand. But the fact is that the technical boys are ahead of schedule. We've decided to bring forward the time of the rocket launching.'

Four days ... Brand thought fast ... time was running out, and he had to complete this investigation before the satellite was due to be launched.

He drew Nick aside. 'I want you to stay here,' he murmured quietly. 'Stick close to Professor Colman — don't let him out of your sight for a moment.'

'Right, chief,' Nick said, and then shot a covert glance at the scientist, and grimaced. 'But I don't think he's going to like it . . . '

'Then he'll have to lump it,' Brand answered grimly.

# 11

## Frost pays the price

Bob Frost was sweating. He sat in a back room of the *Red Bull* in Oakhampton alone with a bottle of whisky . . . and with his fear.

His thoughts were chaotic. His head was muzzy with drink, his pale brown eyes glazed. What a man would do for a woman, he thought dully. For what he'd done, he could lose his job and his pension — and more. And Brand was suspicious. The mental image of prison gates haunted him.

He started out of his reverie. 'Marilyn — ?'

But he was still alone in the room. Marilyn was late. And he began to fret over her lateness. What did it portend? There had been a strange, disturbing quality in her voice over the telephone . . .

He was to meet her at the *Red Bull*,

alone. She'd arranged for a private room there, she'd told him.

Now his watery gaze wandered miserably from the drab plaster walls to the wooden benches and scarred table. He'd never imagined that she'd meant a room like this. A dingy picture of a stag at bay hung crookedly from a nail over the fireplace.

Then the door opened, and Marilyn Martin stood there. Her gaze darted round the room. 'You came here on your own, Bob?' she asked, sharpness in her voice.

'Course I did.' The words slurred off his tongue. He rose unsteadily, reaching for her. 'I thought you were never coming,' he grumbled.

Her painted face was hard. She pushed him back into his seat and laughed shortly. 'You look worried, Bob.'

The fear stabbed him again.

'Marilyn, you've got to help me. I'm in a mess. That pass . . . something happened out at the station. I've got to know who you gave that pass to.'

'Shut up,' she said coldly.

Frost stared at her stupidly, then swallowed. 'Marilyn — ' he began desperately. 'You must help me. If you don't, I'll lose my job. They're bringing in American security officers.'

Her eyes narrowed. 'American . . . ?' Then her voice softened a fraction. She forced a smile as she slid into the seat beside him. 'That's interesting. Tell me about it, Bob. When are they coming?'

'I don't know. It's Rushton's idea . . . ' The name needled his whisky-soaked memory. 'Rushton's friend, the man you gave the pass to . . . what's his name? I've got to find him.'

The redhead stared at him, saying nothing.

'Try to understand,' Frost said urgently. 'I — '

She interrupted him harshly. 'No, You try to understand, Bob! Try to understand this. We're through!'

Frost gaped at her.

'But the money . . . ' he got out finally. 'The money for the pass . . . '

She laughed in his face.

He said helplessly: 'We're going away together . . . '

135

'Are we?' She stood up abruptly, moving to reach the door. He tried to stop her, hold her, and missed her. He almost fell out of his chair.

'Marilyn — !' The name came out as a strangled gasp.

She turned, her excellent figure framed by the doorway, her face set in harsh lines. 'No, Bob, we're not going away together. We never were. You're a prize sucker — and you deserve all that's coming to you. My God, the things I've had to put up with from you! But that's all over now! It wasn't even good while it lasted!'

She laughed again. The door closed behind her. Bob Frost sat alone, stunned.

Then he reached for the whisky bottle; finished it. There was no longer any fear in him. Nothing mattered any more. His dreams had shrivelled and died.

He had the truth now. She had never cared. She had been using him, and he'd fallen for it. God, what a fool he'd been! What a fool!

The thought sobered him. What was there left? Disgrace . . . nothing more.

He was a responsible officer. The security of the station depended on him, and he'd misused that trust. He had betrayed his country for a woman no better than a harlot.

The whisky bottle was empty. It held no more for him than life itself. He grew cold sitting there, stroking the ragged ends of his moustache. His dreams had died, and he knew he couldn't face an inquiry.

Shuddering, he dragged himself to his feet and stumbled to the door. He flung it wide, seeming to hear, as he did so, an echo of Marilyn's harsh, mocking laughter.

He lurched out of the *Red Bull*.

There was now only one thing left for him to do . . . if only he had the courage to do it.

★  ★  ★

'Four days . . . ' Marla Dean echoed. 'That's a tough order, chief!'

She sat on the edge of the bed in her room in the *Wheat Sheaf*, notepad on knee, pencil poised. Simon Brand stood with his back to her, looking down at the window shoppers along the High Street. He swung round, a brief smile erasing the lines of concentration from his forehead. 'We'll cope,' he said. 'Somehow.'

He paced the carpet, deep in thought

'There's one thing we can be sure of. One thing that's absolutely certain. The Martin woman is in this business up to her neck. And it's equally certain that her contact at the station is Frost . . . the Chief Security Officer, no less.' He kicked at the carpet abstractedly. 'These people are certainly well organised.'

He went on: 'I've asked the local police to pick up Miss Martin and hold her for questioning. I'll put pressure on Frost. If I can persuade him to give evidence against her, she may break down in turn and give me some real evidence against Vogel. I'm pretty sure that he's behind everything that's going on around here, but — ' Brand sighed ' — as things stand, I can't prove it.'

Marla said: 'And what about that man

that Kaner told you to watch out for? Wasn't his name Hurley . . . ?'

Simon Brand nodded, and frowned

'It was . . . and we haven't turned up anyone of that name so far.'

He resumed his pacing.

'I've got Nick watching Colman. The professor is the key to the whole show . . . and I'm still waiting to hear from America about the Vogel-Rushton tie-up. There could be something interesting there.' His brow furrowed again. 'The real question is what form will the gang's next move take? Because we can be quite sure they will try again.'

Marla said: 'If you're so sure that Vogel's behind all that's been happening, why don't we do something about him?'

Brand shook his head a trifle irritably. 'I told you, Marla. We've got no proof. No proof at all. And without proof we're helpless.'

'Maybe,' Marla said slowly, 'I could get the proof that we need.'

Brand eyed her sharply. 'What do you mean?'

Marla said: 'Vogel was interested in me.

Maybe I should follow that up.'

Brand shook his head decisively. 'Not on your life!'

He said: 'Have you forgotten that we've established some sort of a link between Vogel and Marilyn Martin? Your interest in that young lady very nearly got you killed, and it's my bet that it was one of Vogel's henchmen who pulled the trigger on you. We're not running that risk again! Vogel and his kind play for keeps!'

Marla protested: 'But I'd be all right. Really I would. You'd know where I was.'

'Meaning you'd be calling on Vogel —?' Brand shook his head again. 'It wouldn't achieve anything. Not a thing.'

'But you can't say that. It might,' Marla insisted. 'I might see something, or overhear something . . . '

She didn't feel happy about calling alone on Mr. Vogel; she could still feel his eyes crawling over her. But she was loyal to Brand and, if there were the slightest chance of getting results, she'd go through with it.

'No, Marla,' said Brand.

'I might even be able to charm

something out of Vogel,' Marla said.

'I'd sooner think of you charming a rattlesnake,' Brand said. 'Once and for all, Marla, the answer's no!'

★   ★   ★

But, half an hour later, Marla took the lift down from her room and sought out Oakhampton's chief garage. There she hired a car that she drove out of town over the West Bridge, and then turned south along the main road.

Nick had located Vogel's residence with a local house agent's help, and now Marla had no difficulty in finding it.

The house was big, set in its own grounds behind a screen of tall trees. Once she had entered the drive, she was completely cut off. A tiny shiver of fear ran through her body. She had to steel herself to drive up to the massive doorway. She was disobeying Brand's orders. She hoped the results obtained would be her justification.

She cut her car's engine and stared at the door. She sensed an aura of menace.

It was as though the eyes of Boris Josef Vogel rested on her already . . .

Marla Dean shuddered. She caught up her handbag, feeling the hard outline of the small .32 revolver inside. It gave her courage.

She went up the stone steps . . . and the door at the top of them slowly and silently opened.

There someone waited in the deep shadows . . . to greet her.

★　★　★

Doctor Fenwick was curious.

The portly, ruddy-faced medico of International Communications thought it strange, considering the intense security check-up now going on, that Frost should be so hard to find. An unusual type, Bob Frost . . . he wasn't in the right job at all!

Fenwick, puffing a little, walked up the concrete path leading to the security officer's prefabricated bungalow. He wasn't in his office, and nobody seemed to know exactly where he was. The

142

station covered a large area; but it was strange just the same.

There was no movement from within the bungalow. No sound.

Fenwick jabbed the bell-push with a fat thumb. Frost should have married, he thought. He needed a stabilising influence. The portly doctor listened to a bell ringing somewhere inside the bungalow, but no one answered.

He was about to turn away, but then, on impulse, he tried the door and found it unlocked. That really surprised him. Frost was a man he thought of as living behind perpetually locked doors. That would have been in character.

Fenwick pushed open the door and called: 'Frost . . . ?'

He received no answer. He hesitated a moment, and then moved across the hall of the bungalow. The living room was empty and so was the kitchen.

The door of the bedroom was locked.

The curiosity of Doctor Fenwick increased. He rapped on the door and called Frost's name loudly. Again there was no answer. Why should a man bar the door of his bedroom but leave the front door of his bungalow unlocked?

Fenwick dismissed the idea of Frost being closeted in his bedroom with a woman. Frost was the secretive kind; he would never bring a lady friend openly on to the station.

The doctor paced back across the hall of the bungalow, grumbling to himself. He went out through the door. He walked round the bungalow, trampling on flowers, until he came to the bedroom window.

He looked inside. And he gasped. He couldn't help it.

There he was — Bob Frost. There, in the bedroom. Fenwick could see him.

Frost had hanged himself. His snarling, empurpled face was livid and terrible.

# 12

## Marla in peril

'Well now . . .' wheezed Boris Josef Vogel. 'I'm delighted to see you, Miss Dean. Please come right in . . .'

Marla allowed him to guide her over the thick carpet to a deep settee. They were alone in the room, and heavy drapes deadened all sound.

Vogel chuckled fatly. 'I like a little comfort — and I can guarantee we shan't be disturbed. Just make yourself at home. You'll take a drink?'

'Thank you.' Marla tried to keep her voice casual.

Vogel waddled over to a long cocktail cabinet and returned with two brimming glasses.

He didn't take his eyes off her for a moment. She found it impossible to relax under such concentrated concupiscence. She sipped her drink and carefully placed the glass on the small table beside her — along with her handbag.

She wished that she hadn't come.

There was an aura about Vogel that sickened and frightened her. He was one of the most physically repellent men she had ever met. Suddenly, she had an almost frantic need to get out of this room and away from him. But she fought it. She had come here of her own free will and against Brand's better judgment. She couldn't cut and run now.

Smiling, Vogel offered her a cigarette from a gold casket. Marla accepted the cigarette gratefully. She blew out a plume of smoke, and said:

'When we met in Oakhampton, you indicated that you might find a place for me in your organisation . . . '

'And why not, Miss Dean?' Vogel's voice was a smooth purr. 'I think you might fit in very well.'

He sat down beside her on the settee; one of his grossly fat hands lightly touched her blonde hair, then slid down to a shoulder . . .

'Yes, indeed,' he purred. 'I think you

might be very suitable for what I have in mind.'

Marla brushed his wandering hand with the glowing tip of her cigarette. The hand scuttled back out of danger like an obscenely bloated creature with a life of its own, and Marla felt fleetingly grateful to 'Headline' Harry Levin, Simon Brand's newspaper columnist friend who had taught her so much.

For, in dealing with Harry, she had learned a lot about fending off unwanted passes. Not that she'd ever had to brand the hand of the journalist. She hadn't. Harry's passes were almost invariably playful.

Not so Vogel's.

This man wasn't playing. He meant business. And he wasn't easily discouraged.

The hand that had scuttled out of danger now came back again: but more roughly and aggressively this time. Marla resisted; squirmed away. And Vogel's treatment of her got rougher than ever.

Suddenly, Marla was having to fight him off. She was flung back upon the couch. She struggled furiously. 'Let me go! How dare you! I — '

But Vogel was strong.

'You'd better be reasonable!' His breath was hot in her face. His fat hands pawed and pried. 'You'd better behave, or — ' he spat the last words out as she tried to wrench away ' — or you won't get out of here in a hurry!'

He forced her back down again: down upon the yielding couch.

'Do you think I don't know why you came here?' He laughed at her struggle to defend herself. 'Of course I do! You came here to spy — to find out all you could about me. Well, you're finding out, aren't you, my dear? Aren't you — ? And you'll know me better before this day's over, that I promise you!'

Now Marla summoned her last ounce of strength to her assistance and fought silently and desperately to fend off Vogel and free herself . . . in vain.

For, suddenly, all Marla's strength was gone. All her resistance ended. Suddenly, the room was darkening and lurching round, and she was sinking down, down into a nauseous sea of black unconsciousness.

It seemed to happen in an instant; inexplicably. One moment she was fighting hard, and even winning. The next she was completely helpless.

Clutching desperately at the rational, on the brink of utter irrationality, she got out: 'Drink . . . ' the word was slurred, sleepy ' . . . you doped my drink . . . '

It was the only explanation.

And Vogel smiled down at her, a savage, red-lipped smile.

'Of course, my dear . . . ' he said, and his voice seemed to echo hollowly through time and space. 'Of course, my dear . . . '

And then he said: 'I am the one man in the world who always wins — no matter how. I am the one man in the world who always wins . . . and never loses . . . '

# 13

## A blonde for Hurley

Half an hour before, Melanie Bourne had groped her way up out of very deep sleep.

Somewhere, a bell jangled stridently.

Unwillingly, Melanie Bourne opened heavily-lidded eyes and mechanically groped for the alarm clock on the bedside table. A grey light filtered through the curtains at the windows of her bedroom. It must be very early, she thought, confused, and then discovered that the alarm clock she was groping for had long since stopped. But the strident bell went on ringing.

Melanie Bourne really began to wake up then.

It was evening, not morning after all. She remembered the sleeping tablets Doctor Fenwick had given her. They must have been very potent. And it was the telephone jangling, not the alarm clock or the doorbell. She began to revive as she moved through the hall to pick up the receiver.

'Yes . . . ?'

'Mrs. Bourne?' The voice over the phone was harsh. It sounded staccato. 'My name is Marilyn Martin, Mrs. Bourne. I'm sure you would like to know who was responsible for your husband's death. Well — *I* know. And I'm prepared to do a deal with you.'

Melanie was shocked into full awareness. This woman knew the identity of Peter's murderer . . . ?

She said urgently: 'Tell me! You've got to tell me!'

Marilyn Martin laughed. 'It's not as simple as that! I'm in trouble: on the run. I need money quickly. As much as I can lay my hands on.'

'I have about three hundred pounds in the house,' Melanie said.

'Is that all?' The voice held disappointment. There was a pause. Then: 'Well, I suppose it will just have to do. Bring the money with you, and meet me at Kit's Tor. You know it?'

'I know. It is not far from the station.'

'Kit's Tor,' Marilyn repeated. 'In half-an-hour. And tell no one. Understand?'

The line went dead.

Melanie Bourne slowly lowered the receiver. A fierce light burned in her eyes. It was always possible, of course, that the call was some sort of a hoax. But she didn't believe it. She didn't want to believe it.

She dressed quickly in a lilac-coloured frock and white coat. She went to the bureau, found the banknotes lodged there, folded them, and thrust them into a pocket. She set off for the rendezvous.

Something like this was what she'd been waiting for: a chance to avenge her husband's death. She had had no other purpose in remaining at the research station. She would make quite sure that her husband's murderer paid for his crime. After that — her future was blank.

It was growing dark as she left the research station through the main gate. Mist was creeping over the Moor. She half-ran through the bracken towards the shadowy mass of Kit's Tor.

By the time that she reached it, the last glimmers of daylight were almost completely gone, and the mist swirled eerily. Melanie Bourne stood stock still, listening, and peering around her.

Then, somewhere ahead, there was sudden movement. A shape began to detach itself from the surrounding mist. 'I am here with the money, Miss Martin,' Melanie said boldly.

But the next instant fear caught in her throat.

The shape coming at her out of the mist was too big and too bulky for that of any woman. And now it had finite form. It was a man. A big man in hat and raincoat who lunged at her purposefully. She had been tricked! She —

She turned, and she ran.

But she did not get far. There was no escape. The man came after her. He overtook her with ease.

She felt a hard hand fasten on her shoulder. It wrenched her round. She staggered, off-balance. She had a terrifying glimpse of mean eyes, a grim mouth.

And then the man struck.

His fist exploded against the side of her head. It was a punishing blow.

And Melanie Bourne pitched sideways into the bracken.

★  ★  ★

It was Hurley who had clubbed Melanie Bourne down with his fist. Now he crouched by her side. Swiftly he went through the pockets of her white coat. He found the banknotes and stuffed them away in his wallet. After that, he paused, motionless, for a moment.

He stared down at the unconscious girl. Young, lovely . . . blonde. He felt a need for feminine company someone to help pass away the boring, inactive hours.

He reached for her.

He picked her up effortlessly. He slung her over his shoulder and walked away through the mist. He did not have to walk far.

Soon he came to a tumbled mass of huge boulders, and, parting bushes and bracken, to the carefully concealed entrance of an underground cave.

He carried Melanie, still unconscious, inside. And, as he did so, another man started up and wheeled around from where, at the far end of the cave, he had been maintaining watch over a small, metal-clad television set.

'*Blimey* . . . '

This second man, the speaker, was weedy and thin. A hand-rolled cigarette stuck to his lower lip and, getting up from in front of the television screen in a hurry, he had snatched up a submachine-gun. Now he held the weapon loosely — and stared.

He stared first at Hurley, and then at the inert Melanie, and then back at Hurley again.

'*What the hell* . . . '

He said: 'You gone crazy, Hurley, bringing a broad down here . . . ?'

Hurley swung Melanie down on to a camp bed set in the shadows. He said: 'We've got to keep this one under wraps until we've finished our business here. Those were my orders. She's seen too much . . . '

His hands lingered on the unconscious Melanie.

'Hell!' The little man's eyes shied away from Hurley's hands. He turned on his heels in sudden disgust. He flung back over his shoulder, 'You have to, I suppose. But I don't want no part in it!'

He walked to the other end of the cave and ostentatiously busied himself with the small metal-clad television set. And Hurley laughed, deep in his throat.

Then, suddenly, he slapped Melanie's face — hard. He slapped it again. And again. She started to moan protestingly. Her head slewed around. Then her eyes came open.

She stared straight up into Hurley's face, and flinched at what she saw there.

Hurley laughed again: a blood-chilling sound. He said: 'Aren't you going to ask where you are, baby? It's usual.'

Frightened, she stared around her.

'You've got yourself into a hole, baby,' Hurley said. 'That's just what it is . . . ' His voice hardened. 'And you're going to have to make the best of it.'

Melanie shrank back. The other man in

the cave was pointedly ignoring her. She had only herself to rely on . . .

She launched herself at Hurley, ripping his face with her nails. She brought up her knee, savagely.

Hurley held her easily. He was a powerful man. She squirmed under his hands.

'I like a girl with some spirit,' he said.

Melanie fought. Hurley's eyes gleamed.

'My, my,' he said thickly, 'you certainly are a little spitfire.'

Then he flung her back.

Melanie started to scream.

The small man in front of the television set flinched at the sound.

He half-turned, hesitated, then slowly sat down.

He kept his back to Hurley and to Melanie.

The girl was still screaming.

★ ★ ★

Simon Brand went up the steps of the big house with cold purpose in every movement. His broad mouth was set in a firm line. His blue-grey eyes held a wintry gleam.

His lean body was taut, expressive of a deep-seated anxiety. Marla had come to this house against his express instructions, and she had not returned. He wanted to know why. He hammered on the door with the heavy iron knocker and waited, easing his Luger free in its shoulder holster.

He was very worried.

There was a close-knit relationship between the members of Simon Brand's staff. All for one and one for all was the unwritten maxim. And there was a long-standing affection between Marla and himself. He was in no mood to listen to fairy stories.

Marla's hired car had been found parked outside the *Wheat Sheaf*, but no one had remembered seeing the driver who had brought it back to the hotel, and Marla had not reported. She carried a gun and knew how to use it, and she wouldn't have been taken without a struggle. Brand was afraid for her.

It was time to face Boris Josef Vogel . . .

The door of the big house opened. Brand shouldered his way past a short, grey-haired man in butler's dress, contemptuous of protests. His eyes raked the hall ahead, and darted up the stairs. The butler tried to lay a restraining hand on Brand's arm, and was sent reeling for his pains. He recovered, and darted around the detective. He put his back to a door, and spread his arms to bar the way. 'No!'

Brand hit him, and burst into the room beyond. But just over the threshold he pulled up short. There was only one person in the room. Not the two people he had half-expected and certainly hoped to find here. There was only one of them . . .

Vogel.

And the gross, gargantuan cartel king and financier was staring at him in considerable surprise. 'What on earth . . . ?'

The short, grey-haired butler picked himself up from the floor of the hall and limped into the room, glaring at Brand.

'I'm sorry, sir,' he told Vogel, 'but this person said — '

The detective interrupted, and harshly. 'I think Mr. Vogel knows who I am. We may not have actually met before, but we've certainly brushed up against each other in the past. And I think Mr. Vogel knows why I'm here.'

He clipped his words.

'My name's Simon Brand, and my secretary came to this house several hours ago, and she hasn't returned.'

'No . . . ?' Vogel's deep-pouched, heavy-lidded eyes widened a trifle. 'That's bad, isn't it?' He even managed to sound concerned. 'No wonder you're worried. You think she's met with an accident? The amount of traffic on these roads is something I don't care to contemplate.'

'I'm not worried about an accident,' Brand returned bleakly.

'No . . . ?' Now Vogel looked puzzled. 'What then?'

But Brand wasn't deceived.

The two men faced each other. The financier, immaculately groomed, his deep-set eyes casting an aura of great power. The detective, more than a head taller, muscular body tensed like that of a panther about to spring. Their eyes met. Wills clashed.

Brand said harshly, 'You're not denying my secretary was here?'

'Of course she was here. Why should I deny it? She was here in this very room only a short time ago.'

'And — ?' Brand asked dangerously.

Again Vogel contrived to look puzzled. 'I don't know what you mean. She left. Is that what you mean?'

Brand's mouth was grim. He said abruptly, 'You're not fooling me at all. I'm going to search this house.'

And, despite Vogel's protests, he did. He searched it thoroughly — to no avail.

Marla definitely wasn't there; not any more.

Marla had been spirited away.

★   ★   ★

Ice-cold with anger, Brand left at last, the sound of a mocking gurgle of laughter from Vogel loud in his ears.

'I hope you find her, Mr. Brand. It must be very worrying for you.'

It was that all right.

Brand drove fast to reach the Moor. He drove dangerously fast, with the mist thickening all the while. The sharp needle of desperation pricked him.

Marla was Vogel's prisoner. He was certain of that. But where was she being held? He could only guess, and pray he was right, and pray for something else, too.

As he drove furiously into the mist shrouding the Moor, he prayed for Marla's safety.

# 14

## Brand hits hard

Mist swirled round the high tors and lay like a grey pall over gorse and heather. Visibility was five yards. Brand pulled his car off the road and left the lights switched on. He loped across rough ground, searching for landmarks. He came to the place where — ages ago, it now seemed — he had found the hidden televisor. He approached it warily.

Yes, the televisor was still in position, its single Cyclops' eye of glass peering in the direction of the mist-dimmed, distant lights of the research station as it slowly tracked through a repetitive arc, forward and backward, ceaselessly, endlessly.

Brand crouched down and minutely examined the ground behind it. And this was why.

The televisor must be regularly maintained and serviced. A man must come here to do it. And it was better than a ten to one chance, Brand thought, that he came from the place where the televisor's signals were being received: the secret, hidden place which must exist somewhere on the Moor where an unremitting, clandestine, round-the-clock watch was kept on the research station and all that was happening there.

All that being so, Brand thought, there must be tracks between one point and the other: tracks which, if he could only find them and follow them, would lead him inevitably to the secret, hidden outpost of the enemy.

And find them he did.

It wasn't easy. Nor was it something accomplished all in a moment. It took quite a time.

The televisor was obviously approached with extreme caution by the man sent to service it. Great care had been regularly exercised to avoid leaving tracks, and the average eyes of the average person would never have found a trail to follow.

But Brand was not 'average.' Far from

it. He was by no means 'average' in any respect.

So it was that, little more than an hour later, Luger in hand, Brand stealthily and silently parted the bushes and bracken that concealed the entrance to the enemy's secret cavern.

He had found it!

He tensed himself, took a deep breath and — the next instant — he hurled himself through the entrance and into the cave.

He hurled himself straight into action!

A little man whirled around from in front of a small, metal-clad television set as Brand rocketed into the cave.

Everything happened at once.

In the same moment that Brand caught another flash of movement on his left out of the corner of his eye, the little man saw Brand and lunged for a submachine-gun which rested against the rocky wall. But he never reached it. He hadn't a chance. He was fast, but Brand was faster.

The Luger in Brand's hand bucked and barked — twice. The little man was flung backwards by the bullets' impact. He crashed to the ground with a shattered shoulder, and he took the television set down with him in an explosion of glass.

Then Brand was wheeling. Wheeling left.

There, starting forward out of the shadows, gun in hand, was a big man in a grey suit. And beyond, deeper in shadow, was a camp bed, a sprawled blonde.

'Marla!'

A murderous fury gripped Brand as he fired.

His bullet took the gun clean out of the other man's hand. The weapon spun through air uselessly, and smashed against a wall.

The big man jerked back, his hand streaming blood, and there was naked fear on his face as he saw Brand's expression.

'No — !'

Brand's trigger finger had tightened again. His mouth was rock hard. His eyes were terrible. He would have killed without qualm, without thought.

'Mr. Brand!' But it wasn't Marla's voice. 'Thank God you're here!'

Brand regained control of his emotions as he recognised Melanie Bourne. He stepped forward and jammed the muzzle of his Luger into the stomach of the big man. 'Back up!' The command was harsh, flat and deadly. 'Back! Get back against the wall!'

The big man obeyed with alacrity. He had looked Death in the face. He was trembling.

'Mrs. Bourne, are you all right? Is Marla here?'

'Yes ... No ... ' Melanie rose unsteadily to her feet. Her face was bruised and her lilac-coloured dress was mud-stained and torn. 'I haven't seen her at all.'

Face grim, Brand leant his weight on his Luger, and said savagely to the big man on the other end of it, 'Talk fast — what have you done with my secretary?'

The big man sweated.

'She isn't here. You're making a mistake, Brand. We haven't touched her.'

'His name is Hurley,' Melanie said suddenly. 'And I think he has another gun.'

Brand's free hand went through Hurley's pockets. Hurley, the man who had brought Marilyn Martin from London . . .

Brand fished out a small automatic and gave it to the girl. 'If either of these two makes a move, don't hesitate to shoot!'

Melanie bared her small teeth in a sudden and savage smile. 'I'll do that all right.'

Brand turned away and made a swift search of the cave.

The first thing he found was a high-powered rifle fitted with a telescopic sight. Was this the gun that had killed Ben Weller? Brand thought so. The police would have the job of matching bullets. But he didn't doubt that they would be successful.

Next he found a cylinder that looked like a compressed air unit: identical with the one he had inspected in the space cone. But a brief examination proved this cylinder to be something more lethal: more deadly. And it took Brand no time at all to reach the conclusion that this was the murder weapon that had been used against Peter Bourne!

Yet another piece of the puzzle dropped into place!

But he still wanted to know: *Where was Marla Dean?*

Melanie Bourne held her automatic straight and true. Her voice was tight. 'Are these the men who killed my husband, Mr. Brand?'

'No.' Brand felt immense sympathy for her. She was going to be deeply hurt again if ever she learned the truth . . .

The little man with the shattered shoulder was moaning. 'Doctor . . . doctor . . . I gotta see a doctor!'

Brand made an abrupt movement with his gun.

'Help him up,' he said to Hurley. 'Get him on his feet, then get outside, the pair of you. I'm handing you both over to the police.'

Brand marched his prisoners through the mist towards the research station. The security guards there could hold them temporarily. He had to get back to the big house, and Vogel. And this time the cartel king would tell him what had happened to Marla. He'd have to! Brand was grimly prepared to go to any lengths to get the truth.

As they neared the main gate of the research station, a black saloon car roared out, travelling at speed, and Brand frowned.

He thought be recognised the man in the back . . .

★ ★ ★

Half an hour earlier, the guard at the main gate of Intercontinental Communications had settled down with a cup of tea and an evening paper. The gatehouse was warm and well-lighted; outside the mist thickened. He had not anticipated many visitors that night.

When he had heard a car approaching, he had opened the door and peered out. Beyond the steel-mesh gate was a black saloon, engine running. A broad-shouldered man with a snap-brimmed hat climbed out.

'United States Security,' he said, speaking with an American accent. 'I guess you're expecting us?'

The guard hesitated. He'd heard rumours about American security men coming to the station — but he'd had no precise instructions.

'You've got passes, I suppose?'

The man in the snap-brimmed hat shook his head. His tone was mild. 'Same old muck-up, I reckon. You'd best call your head man.'

The guard coughed. He didn't like to explain that the station's chief security officer had recently committed suicide . . .

The American shifted a wad of gum from one side of his face to the other.

'Rushton's the man who called us in. You could contact him.'

'Yes, I'll do that. Wait a minute.'

The guard had stared through the swirling mist. There was a second man in the car, behind the wheel. He stepped into the gatehouse and used the phone.

'Mr. Rushton? There are two men outside. American Security. Do I let them through?'

He waited. Rushton's voice came back.

'Hold 'em right there. I'm coming down myself.'

The guard went back to the gate.

He said, 'Mr. Rushton will be here in a few minutes.'

'Fine.'

Then the driver of the saloon stepped from the car. He, too, was a big man wearing a snap-brimmed hat.

The mist eddied round him.

'It's okay, Hank,' the first man drawled. 'Rushton's on his way.'

The guard took a step nearer the gate. 'A dirty night — '

It was a mistake. A powerful hand plunged through the steel mesh of the gate and fastened around his throat, cruelly choking him. The muzzle of a gun buried itself in his stomach.

'Freeze, buddy!'

The man called Hank reached for the guard's keys and unlocked the gate.

He edged through the gap, slugged the guard and dragged him inside the gatehouse. He tied him to the desk quickly and efficiently and rammed a gag into his mouth.

The first man drove the car in and reversed it for a quick getaway. Footsteps sounded, echoing strangely in the mist. Rushton, wearing a jacket over his check shirt, came hurrying towards them.

He said: 'You're not — '

'That's right, Rushton,' Hank said gently, 'we're not!'

The first man prodded Rushton with his gun.

'This is liable to go off and blow a hole clean through you. You'll do exactly as you are told. Understand?'

Rushton stood very still. Even his breathing seemed to be suspended.

Then —

'Yeah, yeah,' he muttered. 'I get it.'

Hank said softly: 'You're taking us to the professor. Any tricks and you're through. Get going!'

Len Rushton swallowed. He moved through the mist with a gun at his back. He thought: Brand's junior partner is with Colman . . . it's up to him. His shoes made lonely sounds on the concrete path.

'Straight to the professor, and no tricks,' reminded the man with the gun.

'Okay, okay . . .'

Rushton hurried. He took the path leading to the prefabricated bungalows, counting the dim, grey buildings. A light shone from behind the curtains of Colman's living quarters; the sound of music came from within. He moved into the porch; rang the bell.

They waited.

The door swung wide, and the dapper, bearded figure of Professor Colman stood in the opening, a smoking cheroot in his hand, glaring at them.

'What is it now?' he demanded testily. 'Can't a man have any privacy? I was just — '

The man called Hank pushed Rushton through the doorway. The man with the gun followed smoothly. Hank closed the door.

Nick rose from a comfortable chair beside the television. He noted Rushton's expression and studied the two hard-faced men behind him. The professor had yet to realise that something was wrong.

'Who are these men?' Colman snapped. 'Explain yourself, Rushton!'

'I'll do the explaining, prof.' Hank moved casually to the television and turned up the volume. 'A friend of ours would like a chat with you. It's just a short ride, and we've got a car down by the gate. There's no need to get excited, and nothing to worry about. You're not going to be hurt.'

Nick's hand was in his pocket. He said: 'Professor Colman doesn't go anywhere without me.'

Hank looked at him.

'That so? Who's your friend professor?'

Colman snorted. 'He's no friend, of mine! He's a damned watchdog supplied by that infernal private detective — '

He didn't get any farther, for that was the moment that Rushton moved.

Attention seemed to have switched away from him. He thought he saw his chance to escape. He jumped for the door. He never reached it.

The man with the gun pivoted smoothly, and there was a roaring explosion instantly drowned out by the music coming from the television. Rushton was hurled forward. His face ploughed into the carpet. A dark stain leapt across the back of his jacket.

He did not move again.

But in the same instant, Nick threw himself forward, bringing his hand out of his pocket and holding a .38 Smith and Wesson. Hank stuck out a foot. Nick stumbled. And, smoothly pivoting back to meet him like a precise, well-integrated machine, the other American smashed the gun out of Nick's hand.

'Run for it, professor!' Nick shouted. 'Get help!'

He lashed out with his left hand, fighting desperately. His right hand was numb. A savage blow from behind exploded across the back of his neck. Nick twisted sideways, face contorted in pain. These men were professionals. Ruthlessly they took it in turn to hit him, each striking a nerve-centre, reducing his resistance to zero.

Nick's legs buckled. He fell to his knees. He tried to get up again, but his body wouldn't respond . . .

Hank said: 'You're way out of your

depth, buddy boy. You're not in the big league.'

Nick felt one last savage explosion of pain across his head, and then pitched forward unconscious.

Colman hadn't moved or opened his mouth. He looked at the two men with disgust, still holding a smoking cheroot.

'You filthy thugs,' he said coldly.

Hank smiled a thin smile, and took his arm. 'They both asked for it, prof. Let's be moving.'

Colman stepped outside, into the mist. He had no choice with a man each side of him, urging him on. They moved back along the concrete path towards the main gate.

They saw no one, heard nothing. The mist was even thicker now, giving them perfect cover. Hank pushed the professor into the back of the black saloon and started the engine. The other American slid into the car with him. They drove out of the research station at speed.

# 15

## Vogel offers terms

Brand thought: *Colman!* Something was very wrong. The main gate of the station stood wide open. He darted forward, into the gatehouse and discovered the guard tied to his desk . . . now he was sure it was Professor Colman he had seen in the back of the car.

'Don't worry about these two, Mr. Brand,' said Melanie Bourne calmly. She still covered Hurley and the small man with her automatic. 'I'm not afraid to shoot!'

Brand cut the guard free. He grabbed the phone and alerted Security; he put through a second call to the Oakhampton police, requesting assistance.

One thought stood out vividly in his mind . . . *Nick.* How had they got Colman away from him? He was sick with worry over Marla; the professor had been kidnapped . . . but what had happened to Nick?

He snapped out orders: 'Hold these two till the police get here, and find my assistant, Chandler, quickly. Tell him — ' Brand ruthlessly squashed a mental picture of Nick seriously injured or worse, 'tell him I've gone to the big house. He's to join me as soon as he can.'

Brand ran off into the mist. He located his car and drove furiously, taking risks. It became impossible to see anything after a while; the mist was solid, impenetrable. He ran the car off the road, cursing. He could move faster, more surely, afoot.

He loped across the Moor, stumbling over obstacles. Precious minutes were passing all too speedily, but the mist would delay the gang too. They couldn't get the professor away quickly. He must be in time!

He reached the main road and increased his pace. The big house was not far away. Racing flat out through the mist, he followed the old stone wall to the entrance of the drive.

The black saloon car was parked out in

front of the house. Luger in hand, Simon Brand stepped round the side of the house and found french windows. He blasted the lock with one shot, thrust aside heavy drapes, and strode into the room beyond.

Boris Josef Vogel occupied an oversize armchair. He did not appear to be unduly perturbed by Brand's sudden and dramatic appearance. Behind him stood his three City-suited hatchet men, and seated on the edge of another chair, facing him, was Professor Colman.

Vogel glanced sidelong at Brand.

'Nice to see you again,' he murmured comfortably, 'though I must admit I hadn't thought you'd get here so fast.'

Brand pointed the Luger at him.

'The game's up,' he said tersely. 'The police are waiting if you try to bolt.'

'Is that so? Then the position would seem to be one of stalemate.' Vogel chuckled fatly. 'That is . . . if you want to see the lovely Miss Dean again . . . alive . . . '

Brand's gun-hand tensed. The light in his blue-grey eyes was suddenly cold.

Although he had no idea what had happened to Marla, it was against his code to bargain with criminals. He held his Luger steady on Vogel and his three hatchet men.

'If it comes to a shooting match,' he warned, 'you'll get the first bullet!'

Vogel shrugged.

Then he said: 'The professor is joining my group willingly and of his own choice. With no coercion at all. I just put the facts before him . . . '

Brand glanced swiftly at Colman. The professor complicated the situation. Vogel might well be speaking the truth. He remembered the professor's own words: 'I don't care who runs the show. Why should I . . . ?'

He said tersely: 'And just what are the facts?'

'Rushton is dead, Mr. Brand, so there'll be no more money to come from his organisation in America. Intercontinental Communications is finished as things stand. My organisation is ready to step into the breach, however. So Colman comes to us.'

Professor Colman tugged at his beard with a nervous hand.

'One must be realistic, Mr. Brand,' he said. 'I am a scientist, concerned only to get on with the job. Nothing else matters to me.'

Brand lifted a sardonic eyebrow.

'In that case, professor, I'd better give you a few more facts! The rocket containing your equipment is ready for firing. You have no reason to doubt its success. And success will bring increased government support, British and European . . . so don't fall for Vogel's bluff. I assure you it is bluff, for he will shortly be under arrest! Now let me give you the background . . . '

Brand studied Vogel carefully. The man was too relaxed; he must still have another trump left to play. He concentrated on converting the professor to his way of thinking.

'Two men realised the enormous profit to be made out of your invention. Vogel, representing an international cartel, and Rushton, representing certain American interests. They decided to pool resources and clean up. But Rushton was greedy . . . he double-crossed his partner and grabbed the sole rights for himself. It was that double-cross which led directly to crime . . . and the murder of Peter Bourne and Ben Weller, Bob Frost's suicide, and now the death of Rushton himself. Think about that, professor, when you consider the facts . . . '

Brand used his left hand to extract a cigarette from his case. Luger poised, he snapped his lighter, inhaled.

'But Vogel isn't a man who gives up a fortune easily. He already had an agent in this country, an American named Hurley. Hurley brought his girlfriend Marilyn Martin to the *Wheat Sheaf*. She played her part well. Through Frost's infatuation for her she got all the information Hurley needed . . . and right till the end, when Frost took his own life, he had no idea he was being used.'

Brand shrugged and went on, 'Through Marilyn and Frost, Hurley got at Peter Bourne. Bourne had no real interest in flying; he wanted to be a big business tycoon — and Rushton had turned him down. Hurley promised him a place in Vogel's organisation if he handed over your communicator . . . they had a good plan. The space cone could be controlled manually. All Bourne had to do was land outside the official reception area at a point designated by Hurley. It was as simple as that.'

Brand drew on his cigarette. He was convinced now that Vogel was waiting for something . . . what? The professor was listening, frowning.

'The plan went wrong,' Brand continued. 'The Chief Technician, Ben Weller, became suspicious of Bourne. He tumbled to what was intended to happen. But he didn't think anyone would believe his story. So he decided to execute the traitor himself. That's exactly how he would think of it, executing a traitor . . . he wanted your invention to benefit this country, professor!

'Soon after I arrived, I was sure Weller had killed Bourne. He was the one with opportunity — last man inside the cone before Bourne went up, first man inside when it landed again.'

Brand tossed his cigarette-butt into an ashtray. This armed truce put a strain on him; he could only play for time.

'Weller used an ingenious method, converting an ordinary compressed air cylinder into a gun fitted with a timing device. He switched cylinders on his final test; switched them again after the space cone came down. He had a perfectly legitimate excuse to cover his actions, and no one would take any notice of an air cylinder in his tool-kit!

'He tossed the improvised air-gun over the wire fence when it had served its purpose, expecting to recover it later. But Hurley had seen what he'd done. And there was nothing fortuitous in that. For a long time now, the research station has been under close and continual observation through short-range TV . . . '

The deep-set eyes of Boris Josef Vogel were regarding Brand with keen attention.

'You didn't think I knew about that?' Brand suggested. 'I had it spotted from the moment Weller was shot. Incidentally, Hurley is now in the hands of the police.

And so is his henchman. And they'll talk, Vogel. They'll implicate you!'

Brand spoke directly to Colman again. 'Hurley saw Weller toss the improvised airgun over the fence, and was intrigued. He retrieved the contrivance, and put two and two together. Then he shot Ben Weller to stop him interfering a second time — '

'Not on my orders,' Vogel interrupted abruptly. 'I'd like to make that very clear. Hurley had no orders to shoot Weller, and as soon as I heard what had happened I came down at once. I am opposed to unnecessary bloodshed.'

'Maybe . . . ' said Brand. 'Yes, maybe you are. But you decide what is necessary, and what is not. And your prime object in coming down here was to get your hands on Colman's communicator. Your minions had bungled things rather badly, and you were impatient for results.

'So — ' Brand looked at the professor again. 'Marilyn Martin wheedled a station Security pass out of Frost, and one of the gang raided your safe. But I'd previously effected an exchange, your communicator for a piece of electronic equipment of my own design, and Vogel was back where he'd started . . . '

Brand paused, glancing round the room. The City-suited hatchet men made no move. Vogel looked thoughtful, and poured himself a drink. Colman lit a cheroot.

' . . . So, finally,' Brand said, 'they kidnapped you, professor.'

Vogel dropped an ice-cube into his glass.

'An admirable reconstruction, Mr. Brand,' he grunted equably. 'But just where does it get you? Remember, I still have your secretary in a very safe place — '

'You'll pay for that,' Brand growled, his Luger raised menacingly.

And then the telephone rang, breaking the tension in the room. Brand scooped up the receiver. He listened. He was smiling when he replaced the instrument. One weight had been taken off his mind. Nick was all right.

'Another mistake, Mr. Vogel. My partner has recovered. He'll testify your gunman shot down Rushton. I suppose you'd call that 'necessary' bloodshed? Somehow, I don't think the police will agree with you. But you can take the matter up with them yourself. They are on their way here at this moment.'

He moved forward. He stood over Vogel. His voice hardened. *'Where is Marla Dean?'*

Vogel settled his immense girth more comfortably in his armchair.

'Safe, Mr. Brand. Safe. But there's something you've overlooked, you know. This mist is local. I have a jet plane standing by to fly me abroad . . . with the professor. And once away from here I fancy I'll be able to pull plenty of strings. Somehow, I don't think that you'll be able to touch me.'

He glanced at the gold watch on his wrist.

'In a matter of minutes, a helicopter will land behind this house. That's one reason I moved in here, because of the large flat lawn. And the helicopter is fitted with infra-red, so the mist won't affect us at all.'

He chuckled fatly. His chins wobbled dangerously. 'Your bluff has failed, Mr. Brand! While I hold Miss Dean you daren't move against me!'

Brand's face was set, hiding a turmoil of thought. A helicopter! The financier's last trump! He wheeled on Professor Colman.

'And you, professor? Are you going along with them?'

Colman began to pace nervously, puffing at his cheroot.

Vogel said softly: 'A bargain, Brand. I have no further use for your secretary. I personally guarantee that she'll be returned to you if you make no attempt to prevent our leaving here. In the other event, you will never see her again. Not ever. That I promise you!'

Brand said gently, 'So, professor?'

Colman tugged at his beard.

'No,' he decided suddenly. 'No. I want nothing to do with this business.'

Vogel stopped smiling abruptly. A mean look entered his eyes. 'In that case, Professor Colman, we'll take you anyway. By force. And you'll give me the secret of your invention — don't doubt it. Don't think you'll be able to hold out on me. I have the means to open your mouth!'

Colman glared at him.

The sound of an aircraft engine reached Brand. He stiffened. The helicopter! The heavy droning note changed. It was coming lower; moving in to land.

A tense silence developed in the room. Brand saw the City-suited hatchet men waiting for a word from Vogel. That was all that they needed, and they'd go into action. Brand kept his Luger steady.

The roar of sound died away behind the house. The plane had landed.

'Now, Brand — ' Vogel's voice was laden with menace ' — the stalemate is ended. You must make up your mind. My freedom of movement for the life of Marla Dean . . .'

A pulse beat in Brand's throat. He tasted gall. Marla . . .

'The professor stays,' he said flatly.

Then the door opened, and a man in flying kit walked into the room.

# 16

## Turning the tables

As the door opened, Brand swept Professor Colman back to the wall. He shielded him with his body, covering Vogel and his henchmen unwaveringly with his Luger.

The helicopter pilot moved into the centre of the room. Then — sensation!

Following him, an angry light in her dark blue eyes, came Marla Dean . . . She had a gun in her hand.

Brand felt light-headed. 'Thank heaven, Marla! I was getting worried.'

Vogel looked considerably shaken. Behind him, one of the City-suited gentry went for a gun. A shot blasted through the room and the gun went spinning.

Nick walked through the french windows holding a smoking Smith and

Wesson. He looked tough; vengeful. One of Vogel's other henchmen made the mistake of trying to rush him, and was met by an iron-hard fist which pistoned into his solar plexus. Then Nick chopped him across the Adam's apple with the edge of a rigid hand, and hammered him across the head with the butt of his gun.

The man crashed into a chair. Wood splintered. The chair disintegrated. The man sprawled on the floor, a senseless heap of twisted arms and legs.

'Anyone else like to try anything?' Nick inquired politely.

But none of the enemy moved. Brand's Luger menaced them.

'How about you?' Nick said to Vogel. 'How about doing some of your own dirty work for a change? Come on. Give it a try. You're old enough, and you're certainly big enough.'

But even had Brand's gun not made acceptance impossible, it was clear from the expression on Vogel's heavy features that he would still have declined the invitation — hurriedly.

A glint of amusement showed in Brand's eyes.

'I don't know what's got into you, Nick,' he said mildly. 'I think we'd better have the police here before you go and hurt somebody . . . '

* * *

'Vogel doped me,' Marla Dean said.

She relaxed with a cigarette, alone with Brand and Nick. The police had taken Vogel and all his henchmen away, and Professor Colman had returned to the research station.

'When I woke up, I was alone in a small room, lying across a bed,' Marla continued. 'It was dark in the room because the only window had been boarded over on the outside. I heard voices, one of them Marilyn's, from an adjoining room. That's when I learned about the plan to fly a helicopter back here to pick up Vogel and the professor.

'I still felt pretty groggy, but I managed to get to the window and squint through a crack. I saw a small airfield, and a helicopter waiting. The door was locked. I hammered on it until they came.'

Marla tapped cigarette ash into an ashtray.

Marilyn brought me sandwiches and coffee. She seemed amused, and there was a man with her — the helicopter pilot. He had a gun. They locked me up again.

'I waited hours for my chance. It seemed years! This time the pilot came in alone. Well, I just grabbed his gun, and tied up Marilyn Martin — she was asleep in the next room — and forced the pilot to fly me back. We arrived just in time for the showdown.'

Marla finished her cigarette.

Nick frowned. 'But you still haven't told us how you got the pilot's gun. I'd have thought — '

Marla Dean, blonde and beautiful, stretched herself. Her voice dropped to a sultry murmur, and she winked at Brand.

'There are ways and means, you know, Nick,' she said.

★  ★  ★

From the blockhouse, the rocket looked like a minute silver bullet poised on its concrete apron.

Simon Brand, Nick and Marla watched anxiously through a slit in the thick protecting wall. Professor Colman had invited them to be his guests at the launching, and Kaner had agreed to wait for Brand's final report . . .

'A job well done, Brand.' The dry, old voice on the telephone conveyed warmth — and asperity. 'I suppose I must wait now until this blasted rocket goes up. Can't see you missing that. Well, you deserve to see the culmination of all your good work.'

The countdown had started. 'Fifty seconds . . . forty . . . thirty . . . '

Nick remembered the young R.A.F. pilot he had met. Alone in a silver spacesuit, strapped into the nose of the rocket, what was he thinking as the seconds ticked away?

Liquid oxygen and alcohol fired the motor. A great gout of flame was spat out. The roar echoed over the concrete and set the very air vibrating. Marla covered her ears.

'. . . Four . . . three . . . two . . . one . . .'

As the noise of the rocket motor reached a deafening crescendo, Brand found himself holding his breath.

'Zero! *Rocket away!*'

Slowly, impressively, the silver bullet rose into an azure sky. Fire spouted from its tail and spilled over the concrete apron. The rocket gathered speed — lifting . . . lifting . . .

Its thunder died away, and left an impressive silence as the rocket soared skyward.

Professor Colman strode up and down the control room, scattering sparks from his cheroot. 'We'll know for certain that everything's running smoothly in a few minutes,' he muttered. 'The pilot will be recovering from the take-off.'

The minutes ticked by. Slowly. Each was an eternity.

The second-stage rockets fired on schedule. Then the third stage.

'Any minute — ' Colman said tautly.

The radio crackled to life, and the voice of the spaceman came through loud and clear. 'I'm fine. Never felt better.

196

Everything's working well.'

He rattled off a series of instrument readings.

'Earth looks like a green-brown ball covered with cottonwool. The sky is blue-black. It's wonderful!'

More readings.

'Approaching point of ejection. Slightly off course. Am about to fire manual rockets to correct.'

A pause.

'Manuals fired — on course again.'

Brand's thoughts travelled from the loneliness of the spaceman in his tiny capsule to the loneliness of Melanie Bourne. He felt overwhelming sympathy for her. What was she going to do with her life now?

The radio crackled again. 'Am about to eject R/T satellite.'

Colman plucked at his beard, pacing faster. He was like an excited schoolboy.

Then — *'Satellite ejected!'*

Colman quivered like an arrow in the gold.

'Now — ' he said, ' — now — now comes the final test.'

They all waited — tensely.

**DEATH NEVER STRIKES TWICE**

**John Glasby**

Suspecting his wife Janine of having an affair, businessman Charles Jensen hires private eye Johnny Merak to follow her. Merak learns that Jensen had divorced his first wife Arlene — who has since disappeared . . . Convinced that Jensen had arranged Arlene's murder, Arlene's sister, Barbara Winton, also approaches Merak to investigate. Ignoring warnings to drop his investigations, he's knocked unconscious, and wakes next to a woman's corpse — a woman who has been shot with his gun. Then the police arrive . . .

# THE CROOKED STRAIGHT

## Ernest Dudley

A mysterious series of factory and warehouse fires was creating havoc, and the police did not appear to be getting on the track. So the *Globe* newspaper hired private eye Nat Craig to see what he could discover. Craig's investigations lead him to suspect arson as part of an insurance fraud, but when two young women are found brutally murdered he soon realises that the arson and murders may be connected. But who is the mastermind behind it all?

# ANCIENT SINS

## Robert Charles

When a fifty-year-old human skull was discovered in a lorry-load of sugar beet, it came at an inconvenient time. Breckland CID was fully involved in a three-county police operation, with the targets for Operation Longship in their sights. However, the old wartime mystery could not be ignored. DS Judy Kane was assigned to unravel a tangled skein of ancient sins — but a tortuous trail of lost loves and fiery passions would lead her into terrible danger.

# THE OSHAWA PROJECT

## Frederick Nolan

1945: the War is over. A secret meeting takes place in Oshawa, Ontario between two powerful players in the post-war US Army, Donald Rogers and Mike Rafferty. The fragile alliance between the USA and the Soviets is being threatened by the aggressive outspokenness of one man — Brigadier General George Campion. Rogers enlists Rafferty into plotting Campion's expert assassination, to be funded by the German Reichsbank's abandoned gold reserves. Rafferty accepts reluctantly. But even a war hero can outlive his usefulness . . .